Into the Deep Woods

Book 1 of the Deep Woods Series

Nila D. Bond

Cover designs and illustrations by Mallory Wilson.

For Mom who always listened and allowed me to dream

and

For Mallory who dreams with me and is the inspiration for this story

Prologue

The tiny, old woman sat on a log with her back resting against the giant hickory that was providing shade. Her long, gray dress and knitted shawl kept the evening chill at bay as occasional breezes found their way to the interior of the thick forest. She leaned her head back against the enormous tree trunk and closed her eyes to the surrounding greenery. Her face revealed nothing as she listened to the voices of the ancient trees. They spoke of events in the distant past and of things yet to come. Something was definitely stirring in these deep woods, and the old woman worked at deciphering the messages that were whispered.

Before the light faded completely from the sky, she opened her eyes and whistled a long, low note. A large hoot owl swooped onto the scene and perched on a low-hanging limb a few yards in front of the old woman. She gazed intently at the bird as it made throaty croaks and chirps lasting for several minutes. When the owl fell silent, the old woman answered in an unknown language, while it blinked its eyes and cocked its head. At the conclusion of the conversation, the old woman rose from the log and walked away into the gathering shadows, with the owl keeping pace overhead.

Chapter 1

The silence caused Mark to look up from the comic book in which he had been engrossed.

"Molly!" he called. *Now where has she gotten off to?*

Receiving no answer, he dropped the comic book on the front porch and headed toward the tree house in the backyard, scanning his surroundings for his three-year-old little sister. She couldn't have gone far. Just minutes ago, she had been blowing soap bubbles and jabbering nonstop in the bright sunshine a few feet from where he had been sitting.

"PHILLIP…THOMAS!" he yelled. Their two heads appeared in the tree house window. "Is Molly up there with you?"

"Nope…haven't seen her," Phillip replied giving an uninterested shrug while Thomas shook his head.

Darn…why can't Mom watch her today?

Mark circled the house looking in the bushes and in all of Molly's favorite hiding places. When he was back to where he had started on the front porch, he ran his hand through his close-cropped hair and blew exasperatedly. With a rising feeling of frustration, his eyes scanned the yard once more. *There…what was that?* He took off across the grass and stopped where the thick forest edged the yard. At his feet lay the bottle of bubbles and plastic wand.

Oh…no!

Mark took off into the woods calling for his sister. "MOLLY!" He stopped and listened carefully. *Was that a giggle?* He headed in the direction of her voice. Listening closely, he followed the faint sound of her childish babbling. At times, he paused and waited for her voice to reach him again so that he could track her. *How could the little pest have wandered this far into the woods?*

It had been several minutes since he had heard her jabbering, and he came close to panicking. He craned his neck and looked up at the tall trees while turning in a circle and straining his ears for any sound of Molly. *Please let me find her.*

When the distant sound of her giggles reached his ears, he took off running, frantically calling her name. He burst into a small glade and came to an abrupt halt. Wearing a look of pure delight, Molly stood illuminated in a shaft of sunlight. She joyfully laughed and danced, clapping her hands while chattering to an invisible audience at her feet. Mark breathed a sigh of relief, bounded toward her and picked her up.

"You scared me, you little rascal. Don't leave the yard again, or you're spending the rest of the summer in the house with Mom," he scolded.

"Put me down. Want to dance…see little people? No, Mark…listen… music," she protested frantically trying to struggle out of his arms.

Mark tightened his grip, ignoring her prattling as he strode through the trees back the way they had come. "Oh, no you don't. Back to the yard you go, little missy. Not a word of this to Dad, or I will be in deep trouble."

After several minutes of useless squirming and pleading, Molly gave up and lapsed into silence. From her perch in Mark's arms, she rested her chin on his shoulder and gazed wistfully back into the deep woods. The music, that only she could hear, grew fainter with every step until it faded completely.

Chapter 2

13 years later

The baseball tipped Molly's glove and landed in the grass behind her.

"Keep your eye on the ball!" Thomas said for the third time.

"Like that's gonna help," Molly shot back.

The two were playing catch in the backyard….. or rather, Thomas was playing catch. Molly was playing "chase the ball all over the yard" since she actually caught very few of them. Despite the fact that her brothers played all types of sports and included her as often as possible, Molly was hopelessly unathletic. She threw the ball to Thomas and managed to catch it when he sailed it back toward her. Thomas cheered, and she did a little victory dance, holding the ball in her glove high above her head.

Just then the front door slammed, and Mark emerged from the house with a duffle bag that he tossed through the window of his parked car sitting in the drive. Phillip was right behind him with his camping gear.

"Load 'em up, guys! I'm ready to hit the lake," Mark shouted.

Molly took off running toward her oldest brother as if to tackle him, but he dodged her attack. She rounded on him once again, and he wrapped his arms around her torso and picked her up, leaving her feet dangling above the ground.

"All right, Carrot Curls, I'm leaving you in charge until we get back," Mark said.

"In charge of what? I'm going to be all by my lonesome, and I'll die a horrible death from boredom. My body will be stinking up this empty house when you three morons get back," she sulked.

"Come on, Curly….you know we'd take you if we could, but this camping trip is just for guys…no girls allowed."

And with that, Mark kissed her on the cheek, gave her an extra squeeze and climbed into the car where the other two boys were waiting. Molly stood in the drive and watched until the car was out of sight. She finally turned on her heel and climbed the steps to the porch. She dragged her feet up the stairs, went into her bedroom and carelessly kicked the door closed. She flopped across the bed and stared at the ceiling, already completely bored.

For as long as she could remember, Molly's family had spent summer months at the large, rambling cottage that was located a few miles outside of the small town of Wells Point. It was a great escape from the summer heat of the city. Wells Point was situated in the hills and had a small lake located nearby that was perfect for swimming and sailing. The house had been in the family for years with Molly's grandparents leaving it to the following generations. It was big and breezy with wide sweeping porches and high ceilings that were designed before air conditioning.

The surrounding lawns were covered in green grass and dotted with tall trees that provided plenty of shade. A tree house sat perched in a massive oak at the edge of the yard, sporting a tire swing beneath. The edges of the yard were surrounded by a vast forest that was older than the summer house.

With Mark and Phillip away at college during the school months, Molly only had Thomas around on a daily basis, and that would end this fall when he also went to college. She was dreading the end of the summer when her brothers would pack their things and all head off in separate directions. She was feeling especially miserable being stuck with only her mother for company in this big, old, empty house. She sighed and got up off the bed.

I am so bored. It's too quiet around here.

She picked a book from the stack beside her bed and headed outside. Up in the tree house, it was cool, shady and quite pleasant. She knew better than to whine to her mother about being bored. Her mother would put her to work around the house the minute she opened her mouth. She believed that nothing cured boredom like an endless list of chores.

Molly's attention wandered from her book as she speculated on her upcoming school year. She hoped that she would have a date or two to this year's dances. So far, none of the boys in high school had given her a second look. She really hadn't cared until lately.

I guess I'm not Miss America material, but who is? Surely there are some decent guys out there who are looking for just a normal, everyday, average girl with alien eyes.

The truth was Molly really did have unusual eyes. She was born with one green eye and one blue eye. Most people didn't notice at first, and few commented when they did. She preferred to think that they were her most interesting feature. She tugged at the curly, auburn locks that she kept short for convenience. No one else in the family had a thick head of curls, and she had yet to find a hair product that would tame her wild tresses.

You could lose a few combs in this mess. What I wouldn't give for long, blonde, perfectly straight hair.

With the conclusion of these thoughts, Molly resumed concentration on her book and was surprised to hear her mother call her in to supper in what seemed a very short time later.

As the evening faded into night, she and her mother sat down to their meal. The absence of the boys was all too apparent with more chairs empty at the table than were occupied. Molly's father was a doctor who worked in the city during the week and came up to the summer house on weekends, so his chair was also vacant. She detested being left alone in the house with her mom.

Why can't Dad take some time off? Why does he have to work so much? Surely there are other doctors who can keep the hospital running. I dread the thought of being stuck here with just Mom when the boys are off at college.

"Stop slouching. Sit up straight, and eat your supper," said her mom. "If I am going to take you to the beauty shop and pay for a haircut, you could at least try fixing it once in a while. Why did we even bother last week if you're going to go around with it looking like a fuzzy mop? Could you just once use some table manners?"

Molly made no comment. It wouldn't do any good. Once her mother started listing her shortcomings, there was no stopping her, and Molly had learned a long time ago to keep her mouth shut and just swallow her anger. Her brothers were the shining stars of the family and garnered most of their mother's affection. Molly had always been a daddy's girl and usually sought out her father when she needed a parent's approval or attention. When her father was around, her mother was less critical and more pleasant. His presence calmed the troubled waters and kept the family running on an even keel. On a night like this, though, she was the sole target of her mother's focus and subsequent sharp remarks. She finished her meal quickly and made her escape from the table.

After supper, she took her pillow and a light blanket out onto the screened porch. The four siblings often spent the night out on the sleeping porch, as the old timers called it. The reclining lounge chairs were very comfortable, and she yawned and stretched as she settled into one. The crickets and locusts had taken up their nightly concert out in the yard, and the familiar sounds began to lull her to sleep. Just as her eyelids drifted closed, the faint sound of music floated on the night breeze that came gently wafting across the porch. Molly's eyes flew open, and she strained in the darkness to make out the source of the music. It had seemed to come from the forest, but it was fleeting. She wondered if she had imagined it. After several minutes, convinced that her ears were playing tricks on her, she chuckled softly to herself.

Just one day alone without Homely, Brainless and Useless and I am losing it. It's going to be a long school year when they leave.

Sometime during the night, faint music came again from the forest, and as it ebbed and flowed on the gentle summer winds, its only audience was an old owl sitting in a hickory tree on the edge of the yard. The owl hooted softly in answer before it took flight into the deep, dark forest.

Chapter 3

Midmorning found Molly sitting on the front porch swing idly thumbing through a magazine. She had declined her mother's half-hearted invitation to go along to attend an arts-and-crafts fair several towns away, assuming that the fair would have the usual crochet doilies, beaded necklaces, painted gourds and the like to offer. The idea of trailing behind her mom, up and down endless rows of homemade junk, and then listening to her and the ladies she was meeting at noon swap gossip over lunch, was pure torture.

One hour of that, and I would be pulling out every strand of this "fuzzy mop."

As it was, Molly had planned to cook a big supper to welcome her brothers back. She had pork chops thawing in the sink and all the makings for smother-fried potatoes and a fresh green salad. She planned to top it off with her specialty....a homemade apple pie.

As they are stuffing their faces with my fabulous, gourmet meal, I plan to make them feel guilty for leaving me for two days. They won't get this kind of cooking at college.

Gently swaying back and forth in the porch swing, Molly stared down the road, silently willing her brothers to appear. A cloud covered the sun, and the yard was cast in shade dropping the temperature a few welcoming degrees.

Suddenly, Molly sat up straighter in the swing, and the magazine slid to the porch floor. *Was that music?* She knew she had not turned on the radio in the house. *There it is again...very faint but unmistakably...music of some sort.*

She left the porch and followed the sound across the yard. She paused momentarily at the edge of the forest. When she was three years old, she had wandered into the woods and had become lost, giving her family quite a scare. They had never let her forget it, and since then, she had only strayed into the edge of the dense stand of trees a time or two. She had never been tempted to go further until now. The music grew slightly louder, and Molly stepped into the thicket of tall trees.

It was cool under the canopy of the trees, and the ground was covered by layers of leaves and pine needles. Leaving the yard and entering the forest felt like stepping from one world into another. She paused to get her bearings and to listen for the music. After several seconds, she heard it again. It was a haunting melody being played on a flute, and the sound pulled her deeper into the woods. She could not have turned back even if she had wanted to...not that the thought ever entered her mind.

Thunder rumbled softly in the distance, but the sound did not register with Molly. She was concentrating on following the music. At times, she paused and altered her course slightly through the woods. While jumping across a small stream, she misjudged the distance, and her foot splashed in the water, wetting her tennis shoe quite thoroughly. She barely felt the cold water soaking her foot and paid no attention to the thunder that sounded closer. She walked on, following no path except the one created by the music weaving through the trees. A strong sense of deja vu came over her as she strode through the tall timbers, but her steps did not slow. The land rose and fell in small hills and vales, and after an hour of walking, she crossed a small clearing, startling a pair of deer grazing on summer grass. The thunder was now overhead and was accompanied by forks of lightning that raced across the sky.

Molly came to an abrupt halt under a large tree. She could no longer hear the music. Between the separate explosions of thunder, she listened in vain to catch even the slightest hint of music, but it was useless. The music was lost. With the spell of the melody broken, Molly felt a strong sense of disappointment and loss. Then came the realization that she didn’t know which way to head back home. She looked very carefully all around. There was nothing to indicate which way she had come. She suppressed the urge to panic when she realized that none of her family had the slightest idea where she was or that she was even missing.

No one's coming to my rescue anytime soon.

A particularly loud crash of thunder sounded overhead, and the next moment, the sky opened and the rain began, soaking her to the skin in minutes. The summer day had turned unusually cool, and Molly was feeling a little chilled. Standing up against a colossal tree trunk sheltered her from the rain somewhat but brought with it other dangers.

Death by drowning in the rain or hug a tree and risk getting hit by lightning. Some choice...guess I'd be better keep moving. Maybe lightning has a hard time hitting moving targets.

She walked on through the forest, wincing and cringing each time the lightning and thunder exploded overhead. Eventually, the thunder faded and only the rain remained. As it came down in buckets, she sat down at the base of a huge tree. The thick foliage overhead provided a shield from the worst of the downpour as she wiped the water out of her eyes and tried to survey the surrounding area. It was impossible to see more than a few yards in any direction since the deluge created a curtain that blocked her vision.

As her stomach growled loudly, Molly wished she had eaten breakfast that morning.

It must be past noon. What I wouldn't give for a hamburger.

To entertain herself, she pictured a big, juicy burger from a popular television commercial and hummed the catchy jingle that went along with it. Then, she sang any other song she could think of to pass the time.

After what seemed hours, the rain finally slowed and stopped. Terribly chilled and shivering, she decided that moving would warm her up. She plodded on through the trees moving stiffly.

Surely, I'll come to a road or a path that will lead me out of the woods.

Unfortunately, Molly was heading deeper into the woods where no roads, paths or trails existed. Because the sky remained overcast, nightfall came early, and she finally stopped walking. As the rain frogs began their loud, croaking chorus, the soggy, bedraggled, young girl curled into a tight ball at the base of a tree and instantly fell into a fitful sleep.

At dawn's first light, she was up and moving through the woods once again. She paused frequently and looked around for any landmarks that might seem familiar. Each tree looked exactly like the others; Molly hoped she hadn't been traveling in circles. Because she was feeling exhausted and feverish, she took many breaks to sit and rest. The rain started again about mid-morning. It was hard to tell what time of day it was; the sun had never made an appearance in the gray sky. She found another large tree with low-hanging limbs and thick foliage to sit under….or was it the same tree as yesterday?

At this point, it really doesn't matter.

She was just as lost today as the day before. In a short amount of time, the large raindrops made their way through the leaves, and she was soaked to the skin again…not that she had completely dried out during the night. The temperature was dropping, and her shivering resumed full force. She dropped her head onto her folded arms that were resting on her bent knees and gave into the overwhelming despair. Her tears mixed with the rain that hit her head and streamed down her face. Had anyone been around, they would not have been able to hear her sobs above the sound of the pouring rain. When her tears ceased, she dozed off and on waiting for the rain to end.

The rain did stop sometime that evening, but Molly was unaware. Once again, she had curled into a tight ball between the roots of a tree and had lapsed into a semi-conscious state of feverish shivering. Hours later, the clouds parted, and a full moon peeked through the leaves of the tree. An old owl, perched on the limb above Molly, hooted softly and ruffled its feathers before settling down for the night to stand watch over the sleeping figure below.

Chapter 4

The joyful trilling of a bird reached Molly's ears, and she snuggled down further in the warm, dry bed. The bird continued to sing sweetly, rousing her a bit more. Pulling the covers over her head, she tried to sink back into deep slumber by refusing to open her eyes. Two new sounds reached her ears……a crackling…. and tiny voices softly giggling in amusement. The crackling continued with each of her movements in the bed.

She slowly opened her eyes and stared blankly at the ceiling above her. It took several moments until she could form a coherent thought.

This isn't my ceiling, and this is not my bed.

The bed rustled and crackled as she rose up on her elbows and looked bewilderedly about. Little faces, wearing curious looks, peered at her over the edge of the bed. Since the little faces were not the least bit familiar, Molly presumed she must still be asleep and having one doozy of a dream. She reached her hand out and touched the wall beside her. It looked and felt like bark. The bed underneath her was a mattress that must have been stuffed with dried leaves thus causing the crackling sounds when she moved.

What a funny dream…but I feel wide awake!

With that thought, she pinched her own arm as an experiment and was surprised when it actually hurt. Now she realized that she was truly awake, clean and dry in some stranger's bed. Looking about the small room, she took in the rustic wooden furniture and the cheerful fire, blazing in the stone fireplace. She turned her gaze onto the peculiar, little faces of the children who were silently standing by her bed. They had stopped their giggling and whispering and were staring at her in awe. "Where in the world am I?" she asked out loud.

"Ahhhh…ye are finally awake." The voice belonged to an old woman who had been sitting by the fire whom Molly had failed to notice. She left her chair and came to Molly's bedside. "Shoo now. Ye mothers are probably looking for ye," she said to the little children who all scurried out the door.

"They donna mean any harm, dearie. We donna get many visitors of yer kind, and they were curious. Now donna try to get up just yet. Ye have been very sick the last few days, and ye are going to be weak for a while."

The old woman's face was lined with wrinkles, and she had a motherly way about her as she put her hand to Molly's forehead. Molly discovered that she was weak and exhausted, so she lay back on the bed and allowed the old woman to feel her forehead and peer into her face. "Yer fever's finally gone. That's good. We were all really worried about ye, Rua."

Rua?

"What's wrong with me?" she asked.

"I 'spect ye picked up a good case of fey fever in the woods, but ye are on the mend now."

"Is this your house? …Whose children were those? …How did I get here?"

"What do ye remember, dearie?"

Molly had now noticed the old woman's peculiar accent. It was like nothing she had ever heard before. She had to listen closely to make out what was being said. "I was lost in the woods, and then the rain started, and I thought it would never stop. I think I slept one night under a tree. It's all kind of blurry. Why am I so tired?"

"That's the fever, child. Ye are going to be fine, though. I'll see to that."

"I've got to get home. My family will be going out of their minds with worry." With that panicked remark, Molly sat up quickly and threw off the covers. The room spun around crazily, and she felt as though the bed would pitch her out on the floor.

The old woman pushed her back down on the bed and covered her once more. "Ye are in no shape to leave just yet. Let's get ye well first. A bit of soup is what ye need now."

The old woman headed back to the fireplace, and when Molly opened her eyes, she had returned with a wooden bowl of steaming soup. Had she fallen asleep again? She didn't remember closing her eyes. The food smelled heavenly; she sat up slowly this time. Taking the bowl that was offered, she quickly ate the entire contents, using the wooden spoon the old woman handed her.

Funny dishes...looks like some of that hand-carved stuff they try to sell to city people at the arts-and-crafts fairs.....in fact, everything about this room and the old woman is strange. Where am I? How will I get back home?

With that last thought, she lay back in exhaustion, and her eyes were closing as her head landed on the pillow. The old woman smoothed the auburn curls back from her face, tucked the blanket around her and picked up the empty bowl in Molly's lax hand. "Sleep well, Rua. The questions can wait for the morrow."

The old woman returned to the fireplace and placed another log on the fire. Then, she took her seat in front of the spinning wheel once again. As the wheel spun with a soft swishing sound, she hummed a tune which sounded similar to the melody that had lured Molly into the forest.

Chapter 5

"Molly-y-y-y.......Molly-y-y-y!"

Someone was calling her name from far away. It sounded like one of her brothers. She tried to answer back but couldn't find her voice. She was running and stumbling through a forest enveloped in fog.

"Molly-y-y-y!"

The voice sounded much fainter this time, and Molly ran frantically in the direction from which it came.

I'm here...don't leave me!

The fog was disorienting, and she dashed from tree to tree, vainly trying to catch a glimpse of who was calling her name.

"Over here!" she tried to shout, but no words would come out of her mouth.

I'm right here! Don't leave me!

Molly came wide awake gasping for air with her heart pounding.

Just a dream...it was just a dream.

She sat up in the bed and realized that while the fog-shrouded forest was a dream, her strange bed and lodgings were not. Light was streaming in through small windows, allowing her to take in her surroundings. The modest dwelling was rustic, to say the least, with a small fire still burning on the hearth, while rockers and wooden chairs stood in front of it. A few shelves contained kitchen items, and pegs on the walls held clothing and household articles, such as a broom, a bucket and a crock pitcher. Bundles of dried herbs and hand-dipped old-fashioned candles hung from the ceiling. There was another wood-framed bed in the corner across the room, just like the one she now occupied except it was neatly made up with a colorful quilt. Molly could see several pairs of shoes lined up in an orderly row, tucked just under the edge of the bed. In fact, everything in the room had a designated place with all items in tidy order. The wood floor was neatly swept, and bright rag rugs were placed about. The wall beside her bed, that seemed to be tree bark, was a mystery to her until she realized that the small home was built right up against an actual tree.

As she sat on the side of the bed, it dawned on her that she was no longer wearing her own clothes but was outfitted in a simple sleeping gown made of the most unusual fabric. It was warm, soft and as light as a cloud.

Just then, the door opened without warning, and in the entrance, a figure was silhouetted in the bright sunshine. In reflex, Molly shrank back and held the blanket up to cover herself.

"Ye are up and awake, I see."

The little, old woman stepped into the house, shutting the door behind her. She removed her cloak and hung it on a peg.

"Let's see about getting some food into ye."

The old woman bustled about the room putting food on the table. She went to the fireplace, removed the kettle from the hook above the fire and set it on the table. Lifting the lid, she grabbed some herbs hanging from the ceiling and tossed them in.

"What ye need is a good cup o' tea."

Molly was struck once again by her unusual accent. She continued to sit on the side of the bed and take in her strange surroundings and the even stranger situation.

"Come on, dearie… tea is getting cold."

Molly stood up hesitantly and moved to the table. She took a chair and looked at the simple food laid out. There was a hot, steaming bowl of oatmeal garnished with honey and berries in front of her. The old woman poured some cream on top of the dish, and suddenly, Molly was famished. She picked up her spoon and looked at the woman.

"Go ahead...," the old woman prodded gently.

The dish wasn't oatmeal exactly, but it was quite delicious. While she ate, she contemplated her circumstances. She didn't feel as though she was in danger. If someone had wanted to hurt her, they could have done just that while she was unconscious. Since she was not tied or bound in any way, she was not being held prisoner. She was wearing clean clothes and was being well fed. When she had finished, she sat back and sipped her tea. It seemed to be an herb concoction which, while unfamiliar, was not unpleasant.

"Were you the one taking care of me while I was ill?' she asked.

"Ye were very sick when we found ye in the forest, but ye will be all right now."

"How long have I been here?"

"Ye spent three nights with me."

"I've been missing that long?" her voice rose in slight panic.

The old woman nodded wordlessly and took a sip of her own tea.

Molly felt a strong sense of urgency to get home. Her family would be going nuts with worry. They probably thought that she had been kidnapped and transported out of the state. The news was always full of stories of missing people who met a fateful end. She hoped that when she got home, her parents would be so overjoyed to see her that they would not ground her for the rest of the summer or send her off to boarding school.

"I really appreciate all that you have done for me, but if you will kindly give me my clothes and point me in the right direction, I will be heading on home now," she said.

"Getting back home could be a wee bit of a problem, lass, but we will do what we can to send ye back to where ye belong. In the meantime, ye are safe and sound with us. Things are going to be a bit....odd for ye...for us as well. It's been a long time since we've had one of yer kind in our midst."

Odd...strange ...bizarre. It's all been unreal since I woke up here.

"What were ye doing in the forest?"

"I heard music and followed it until the rain drowned it out...then I realized too late that I was lost."

"Ye are truly rare and special among yer kind if ye heard our music. My people are usually invisible to Galeings."

Galeings?

"Ye have been here before, Rua. So I guess it is no surprise that ye have found yer way to us again. Ye were just a wee little thing the last time."

Molly just sat silently...taking it all in.

Rua? There's that name again.

"I think you've gotten me mixed up with someone else. My name is Molly."

"Everyone calls me Granny. I am the village healer. That is why they brought ye to me."

The name, Granny, fit the little, old woman perfectly. Her white hair was pulled back into a neat bun, and her long dress and shawl were dark and plain. Her bright, green eyes sparkled in her wrinkled face, and she smelled of recently-picked lavender flowers. She had a calm, soothing way about her, and Molly wondered just how old she actually was. Since it would be rude to ask, Molly didn't.

"I was here before?" she asked instead.

"Think back, child. Ye were very young when ye stumbled onto our village during The Gathering. A Galeing found ye and took ye away before much else could occur. It all happened very quickly."

Molly shook her head in disbelief. Some small inkling of a memory was jogged. It had all gotten mixed up in her little mind so long ago, as childhood memories do. She hadn't thought that it was real. While she was denying the reality of what Granny was saying, a small part of her mind recognized the truth.

"Why can't the....Galeings...see you?" she asked.

Granny shrugged.

"They aren't of our world. They canna see or hear us. It is said that they could in the very distant past. Ye are one of the rare ones that can. Again, our music has reached out to ye and brought ye into our world. I donna know why, but there is a reason. I 'spect we will know why in good time. Until then, ye are welcome to stay with us."

It was all just too much to believe. She was among the little people she had seen in the forest? How? It was impossible......yet, here she sat on a chair that felt sturdy beneath her...with a steaming mug in her hand that felt solid and tangible...and tea that tasted real. Her mind struggled with the reality.

"This.....this can't be."

She abruptly pushed back her chair and numbly walked to the only door in the room. She pushed the door open and took several purposeful steps outside. She halted and stared about....taking in the most amazing sight.

Chapter 6

Molly felt as if she had stepped through a doorway into a completely different world and time. The little clearing was filled with structures that made up a quaint village consisting of houses that were built in between the roots of massive trees. Every structure was organic in nature and made of materials found in the forest. Dried grass was bundled and used to make thatched roofs, and the walls of most of the houses were created with large, stacked stones with pine bark used here and there for siding. The doors and windows were framed with large tree branches that were probably medium-sized sticks in Molly's world. Smoke trickled from the chimneys and evaporated in the early morning chill. The scene reminded her of one of several landscapes on a Thomas Kinkade calendar. She craned her neck to look up at the gigantic trees that surrounded the village. Everything was huge. Even the grass at the edge of the community was the size of tall bushes. Molly continued to stare in shock.

It was several minutes before she realized that a silence had settled around her. She brought her gaze down from the giant trees and foliage, to the view directly in front of her. All village activity had come to a halt as the townspeople stood unmoving and gawking at her. Because they looked so unusual, she openly stared back. They all wore simple homespun clothing that was dyed in bright colors and some had embroidery embellishments of colorful flowers and leaves. Their features suggested an elfin race with slightly pointed noses and very pointed ears. Their fingers were long and slender as were their feet which were encased in soft leather shoes. People like this did not exist in her world, except in the movies or TV. Come to think of it...that was exactly how this felt...as if she had stepped onto a movie set.

Molly finally came to her senses and began to feel self-conscious as the silence continued to stretch on. She looked down when she felt a tug on her gown. A small urchin with a curious look on his little elfin face was peering up at her.

"Are ye weelly one of the Galeings?"

Molly could not resist smiling at this delightful little creature. She squatted down so that they were eye level.

"I suppose I am, and who might you be?"

"Eveewon calls me Butternut, miss.....ye have stwange eyes."

Before Molly could answer, a woman stepped forward and whisked the small child away. The villagers slowly resumed their activities, but sidelong glances came her way as they did so. Butternut was the only villager who had spoken to her, and she felt like the proverbial elephant in the room.

"They will warm up to ye in time. The people of Hickory Hollow are really a friendly sort when ye get to know them."

She had not heard Granny follow her outside.

"I don't plan on being around that long. I don't belong here. They know it, and I know it. This can't be real. What did you do…how were you able to bring me here……how is it that I am now small enough to fit into your world?" Molly struggled to ask the nagging question. She felt slightly dizzy and overcome with the idea of it all.

"Come sit, child. We have a lot to talk about."

Granny led her over to sit on a bench in the sunshine outside the house. She disappeared briefly and returned with a steaming mug of tea.

"Here…drink this."

After a few minutes of silence, Granny spoke softly while Molly watched the villagers go about their activities.

"It took powerful magic to transform ye so that ye could be a part of our world. We save that type of magic for when it is most needed. We had to bring ye here to save ye. Ye would not have survived had we left ye in the woods. Since ye had been drawn into the forest by the music before, we knew that was a sign that ye were supposed to come to us."

"I was supposed to come here?"

Granny spoke slowly, choosing her words carefully.

"Lives follow a chain of events, and even though we may not always understand why things happen as they do, we accept them as they come. We listen to the voices of the forest and read the signs that nature sends us. That is how we found ye."

Molly leaned forward with her elbows on her knees and her head in her hands. She was quiet for some time, struggling to take it all in. She felt disoriented and overwhelmed as so many questions crowded her thoughts. When she finally spoke, she sounded calmer than she felt.

"Have other…Galeings…ever been here in your village?"

Granny nodded thoughtfully.

"Hundreds of years ago."

"Hundreds…..," Molly's voice choked off into silence. "Just how old are your people?"

"As old as these forests."

Molly sat very still on the bench. Her eyes took in the scenery around her while her mind tried to accept what she was being told.

Granny rose to her feet. She wrapped a shawl around Molly's shoulders.

"Sit for a while and rest. Donna fret now….everything will come as it is meant to. Ye must regain yer strength."

Granny went inside the house leaving Molly alone to contemplate her situation. There was quite a bit of activity in the small village. A small group of children were playing in the sunshine. Two women were visiting companionably while washing the windows of their cottage. Older children were collecting firewood and stacking it beside the walls of the houses. A man was repairing his roof while a woman sat peeling apples on a bench in front of the cottage. Something that smelled delicious was being stirred in a big pot sitting over a cooking fire. The woman doing the stirring caught Molly's eye and sent a small tentative smile her way. All of the villagers wore the same simple, homespun clothes and shared the same pointed, elfin facial features.

Molly quietly took in everything around her and tried to organize her thoughts. One thing was clear. No matter how improbable it seemed, she was here in this forest village with no way back to her world at the moment.

The children were now playing a game of tag and were running about, to and fro. One child making a mad dash past Molly, tripped and tumbled head over heels. He immediately set up a wail of pain and began crying. Molly instinctively reached out and plucked him up, setting him in her lap. As she soothed his tears and examined his skinned knee, she heard a loud commotion. Looking up from the child, she spotted an angry, young woman making a beeline towards her. The beautiful woman had ebony curls that floated about her petite features, and she moved as gracefully as a dancer on stage. Reaching the bench on which Molly was sitting, she snatched the crying child from her lap. The child responded by wailing louder than before, bringing more onlookers to stand about the two women.

"Ye will not harm our children, Galeing. Go back to where ye came from. We do not want yer kind here."

Even though she spoke in anger, her voice had a musical quality unlike anything Molly had ever heard. Molly opened her mouth in surprise and shut it as she realized that she had no reply. The idea that she would hurt a child, or anyone for that matter, was preposterous. She sat in shock as the baby was handed off to its mother, who shot looks of suspicion at Molly before striding away with the small child in her arms. The beautiful, young woman stared at Molly with hostility for several seconds before finally turning on her heel and walking away.

"It will take some of the villagers time to get past their fears, but it will work out. Ye will see."

Molly turned to look at Granny in the doorway.

"Who was that?"

"She is called Fenella."

"I wasn't going to hurt the child. I just wanted to make sure he was okay."

Granny chuckled quietly.

"Goodness, lass…I know that. Fenella is being a foolish girl. Steer clear of

her for a while and give her time to become accustomed to yer presence."

While Molly contemplated Granny's remark, some of her old spunk returned.

Maybe Miss Ravenhair should steer clear of me.

For the rest of the morning, the villagers pointedly avoided the bench on which Molly sat and refrained from even glancing her way. When Granny called her in to eat at noon, Molly was feeling more alone than ever, and home seemed a million miles away.

Chapter 7

The next few days followed a pattern. Molly rose early with Granny, and they spent the mornings putting the small house in order and doing the necessary daily chores. In the afternoon, they searched the forest near the house for the healing herbs that Granny required. Molly stuck close to Granny and avoided contact with the other villagers. She did not want a repeat performance of the misunderstanding that had occurred with Fenella. Whenever anyone stopped by Granny's cottage for medicines or cures, Molly retired to a chair in front of the fireplace and pretended to be invisible. She was surprised to find it necessary to rest often and fell into bed each night exhausted, sleeping soundly until dawn. The "fey fever", as Granny had called it, really took some time getting over.

Molly wondered where her clothes were and had asked Granny. The old lady had assured her that her clothes were being taken care of until she needed them upon return to her own world. Granny had given her a simple dress to wear, soft leather shoes for her feet and a knitted shawl for when the mornings were cool. Meals in this forest village were simple…freshly-baked bread, cheese, fruit and dishes made with various nutty grains. The forest people harvested what they needed from the surrounding woods and lived very simply.

On this particular day, Molly was sitting and staring into the fire. Granny had left on an errand, and it was nice and quiet in the snug little house. Molly calculated that she had been in the elfin village for approximately 10 days now. Each time she had broached the subject of returning to her family, Granny had answered with remarks such as, "all in good time, dearie" or "when the time is right, the magic will send ye back." Molly had no idea what that meant and was growing despondent and worried that she might not ever return home.

Even though Granny was very kind to her, she missed her family…especially her brothers. She tried to imagine what her family must be thinking of her absence. How long would they search for her? Did they imagine the worst? Were they sitting down to dinner without her each day? As she thought of each of her brothers, Mark, Thomas and Phillip, she pictured their faces clearly and tears sprang to her eyes. She missed them so much. She missed the weekends at the summer house when her father drove in from the city and the family was complete. Would she make it back before the end of summer?

Just then, a loud knock sounded at the door. She hastily brushed the tears from her eyes and went to answer it. She opened the door halfway and looked at the visitor standing in front of the house.

"Who are ye?" he asked.

He was tall and appeared to be a few years older than Molly. He was dressed in homespun garb like the rest of the villagers but carried a quiver full of arrows on his back and a bow over his shoulder. His hair was long and wispy, and his features echoed similarities to the other villagers. With arms crossed at his chest, he leaned nonchalantly in the door frame, and his clear blue eyes stared directly into hers. Molly took her time answering.

"I'm Molly," she answered simply.

"Are ye new to our village?"

"You could say that."

And then a look of understanding appeared on his face. "Ye are the Galeing that I've been hearing about."

"That would be me," Molly mumbled, looking down at her feet.

"I have never seen a Galeing up close before. I thought all the stories about Galeing visitors many years ago were just tales told by the old ones to entertain the children," he remarked while brashly looking her up and down.

"Get an eyeful, Buddy. Today the freak show is free. No ticket necessary!" The words were out of her mouth before she had time to think. She was homesick and tired of feeling unwelcome.

Blue Eyes' posture had stiffened, and he silently stared at her for several seconds. Molly returned his stare and wondered just how stupid she really was to insult one of the few villagers who had bothered to broach a conversation with her. He then broke into a big smile and chuckled in amusement. "I'm not sure what ye said, but there was no doubt about yer meaning. I meant no harm. I am called Elgin, and I need the village healer."

Before Molly could answer, Granny arrived and took charge of the situation. She hustled Elgin inside and sat him at the table.

"The lads and I were foraging in the forest, and we met up with a band of those pesky goblins. They thought to steal our food, but we fought them off. They got a few bumps and bruises for their trouble, they did. I took a mighty lick to the head and donna know if ye will be needing to stitch me scalp."

Granny parted his light brown hair and took a closer look. "Aye, ye have a fine cut, but it has closed on its own. I'll be cleaning it well and putting some salve on it."

While Granny puttered around with her healing salves and such, Molly retreated to her customary place by the fire.

"So, Molly...will ye be coming to the campfire tonight? There will be lots of storytelling, music and drink. It promises to be quite an evening."

Granny answered for the both of them. "We'll be there, and I 'spect to hear the story of how ye bested the goblins....and donna be stretchin' that yarn past the truth, ye rascal."

As Granny turned away to fetch more items, Elgin playfully held onto her skirt to slow her progress and winked at Molly as he did so. Granny reached back and swatted his hand away while saying, "Watch out now, ye cheeky lad. Ye are not too big for me to dust yer britches."

Molly smiled in spite of herself, enjoying this exchange between these two who were obviously very comfortable with each other. When Granny completed her doctoring, Elgin bent down, kissed her on the cheek and sailed out the door.

As the sunlight started to fade from the sky, Molly and Granny donned their shawls and headed toward the middle of town where a big campfire was already blazing. Logs had been positioned around the edges as benches, and other villagers were drifting in that general direction. Warm greetings were exchanged, and folks called to one another in friendly tones. No one acknowledged Molly, but she really didn't mind. Big barrels were being rolled out and tapped, and drinks were being passed around. Elgin spotted them and headed their way just as they took a seat on one of the logs. He sat down next to Molly and stretched out his long legs. He took a big gulp from the mug he was carrying.

"Shall I bring ye a mug, Molly?"

"What is everyone drinking?"

"Well....apple mead, of course."

"What is that?"

"Ye have never had apple mead? Here...try a sip." He handed her his mug.

She turned it up and took a small tentative drink. She grimaced horribly, shook her head and handed the mug back. Elgin just laughed and remarked, "The forest people are known for their skill in making apple mead. We trade barrels of it with other clans when we go to the big Gathering. Many a goblin has received a mighty thrashing for trying to steal our brewing barrels. I guess apple mead is just one of the things that must be really strange to ye."

Molly was so relieved to have someone sympathize with her plight that she felt herself warming to Elgin as they talked. "I guess the closest thing in my world would be beer or wine, but someone my age isn't allowed to drink it."

"What is ye craft in yer village?"

"I don't really live in a village. I just live in a home with three brothers and my parents. When I finish school, I will have a job and my own family but not for a while. I still have to finish high school and then go to college."

"I donna think I understand the ways of yer world. Here we all learn a craft that will contribute to our village. Meadow over there is the best spinner and weaver among us. She teaches the young girls those skills," Elgin said while gesturing with his mug. "Bantry makes most of the furniture in the village, and Granny, of course, is our healer."

Molly looked around for Granny, but she had slipped away to circulate and visit with others. She noticed plenty of glances coming her way from the villagers. Some were hostile while others were simply curious.

"Elgin, why do they see me as a threat? It is so obvious that I am not wanted here."

"Perhaps that unhappy scowl on ye face has them worried."

"I am **not** scowling!"

"Aye...ye should see yer face, Rua....it would sour milk and scare the wee babies, it would," he said with a chuckle.

Reacting as she would to her brothers' familiar teasing, Molly punched him playfully in the arm and began to laugh in spite of herself. It was surprising to realize that her unhappiness with the current situation was causing her to glower at everyone. Of course the forest people would return her resentful expressions with animosity and suspicion of their own. She vowed from that moment on to relax and not to wear her inner thoughts on her face.

"Why are you not put off by me...like the others?" she asked Elgin.

"I suppose I could see more worry and scared on yer face than the others...I could sense something of it as ye gave me a tongue lashing at Granny's door this morn."

"Oh, Elgin....you remind me of my brothers...and I miss them so," she said with a wistful sigh. "Why am I called Rua?"

"Why...it means red-haired," he explained as he tugged on an auburn curl, "and ye have locks to make autumn maple leaves jealous, ye do."

"You are saving my life, Elgin. I felt so lonely and out of place until I met you."

"It's going to all work out, Molly Girl. Granny is working hard to summon the magic needed to send ye home, but for the time being, ye are here with us and safe in our village. The forest people will look after ye....aye, we will."

The musicians, who had been tuning up their instruments, started a vigorous tune and soon the villagers were clapping and singing along. Molly tried to join in as best she could and felt her spirits rising as the evening progressed. Stories and lively tales were told in between songs, and it was evident that many of the stories had been exaggerated for the purpose of entertainment. Bantry, the village furniture maker, seemed to be everyone's favorite storyteller as he was called on more than the others to relate amusing tales. He had a genuine talent for pulling his audience into the story, and the listeners would lean forward so as not to miss a detail; they hung onto his every word.

Molly did not understand everything she heard that evening, but she caught the gist of most of the stories and laughed in delight along with the crowd in all the appropriate places. The villagers sitting closest to her forgot their feelings of unease in her presence and clapped her on the back as they shared in the laughter. They winked at each other in the exaggerated parts, and one lady elbow jabbed Molly good-naturedly when Bantry over embellished a particular part of a hilarious tale. It was surprising how apple mead, entertaining yarns and a campfire created a relaxed atmosphere among the people.

For the first time, she felt a part of the villagers. Of course, Fenella shot some withering glances her way as the evening began, but Molly pointedly ignored her and soon forgot the dark-haired, young lady altogether. Having Elgin sit next to her and treat her normally also helped the others see her in a different light. All in all, it was a grand evening and well past midnight before the party broke up and people started drifting to their homes. Elgin drained his last mug of the evening and walked with Molly toward Granny's cottage. When they reached their destination, Granny was sitting on the bench beside the door with a small self-satisfied smile on her face.

Elgin bowed with a comical flourish and said very formally, "I bid ye a good night and a pleasant sleep, Fair Ladies." He disappeared in the gloom walking a little unsteadily.

"Ye seemed to have made a friend," Granny said to Molly as they went inside.

Molly smiled and impulsively threw her arms around the old lady and gave her an affectionate squeeze. "Thanks for rescuing me from the forest, Granny. I guess I have pretty much been a pain."

Granny returned the hug and replied, "Ah, well....ye have been company for a lonely, old woman....but off to bed with ye now. Ye need rest or ye will have a setback with the fey fever, and that won't do."

The two women retired to bed in short time and almost immediately fell asleep.

The campfire in the middle of the village was now a pile of smoldering coals, and all were in bed for the night....all, that is, but a solitary figure who had watched from the shadows as Elgin walked Molly home and had continued watching until the last candle had been extinguished, darkening the windows of Granny's cottage. As the forest people settled in for the night, Fenella slipped from the shadows. The livid expression on her face was covered by the darkness as she made her way through the silent, slumbering village.

Chapter 8

After the revelry of the night before, the village woke up more slowly than usual. It was late in the morning before people actually stirred from their homes. The buoyant spirits that Molly retired with the night before had stayed with her, and she was humming to herself as she carried wood into the cottage, replenishing the stack beside the fireplace. Granny was sitting at the spinning wheel and noticed her fine mood but made no comment.

A light knock sounded at the door, and they both turned to find a young woman standing in the open doorway. "I could use a bit of help, if ye wouldn't mind too terribly much, Granny," the woman said. "I need to pick the dewberries in the forest while they are ripe, but I need someone to watch the children, or they'll be all underfoot, ye know."

"Molly can watch them for ye, Thistle. Aye, she's a big help to me these days. Run along, Molly, and give her a hand," Granny replied.

Thistle flashed an apologetic smile at Molly and said, "Truly they won't be troubling ye much. They are good lads and lasses, and I shan't be long in the woods."

Molly reached for her shawl and followed Thistle to her house. It was very much like Granny's with the exception of the children. A small girl and boy played with wooden toys on the floor, and a tiny baby slept peacefully in a cradle. "I'll be back before the babe wakes hungry." And with that, Thistle grabbed a basket and bustled out the door.

Since Molly had held several babysitting jobs back home, she was on familiar territory. It had provided her with spending money, and she had built up quite a clientele. Molly sat on the floor and played with the two little ones. At first, they would only gaze at her solemnly, but she finally elicited smiles and giggles from them as the morning wore on. The baby woke and made a few fussy noises, so Molly picked up the infant and plopped him down in her lap. She made cooing noises at the baby to which he responded with little, squeaky sounds of his own. The children were quite enchanting with their tiny, elfin features. They had exotic eyes that tilted up at the corners, and their tiny noses and ears came to rounded points on the ends. Thistle had been standing in the doorway for several minutes observing the domestic scene before Molly noticed.

"Ye look very much the mum with my three wee ones. Do ye have babies of yer own?" she asked kindly.

"Goodness, no...but I hope to one day."

"May ye be blessed with a warm hearth, a good man and many children, Molly dear."

She spent the next hour helping Thistle feed the children and put them down for naps. After Thistle nursed the baby, she let Molly burp him and rock him back to sleep. The young women then treated themselves to bowls of fresh berries with heavy cream, and Thistle gave Molly a lesson in basket weaving. Molly was a natural and soon had completed a small basket on her own with Thistle's assistance.

When the day wore on to evening, she bid her new companions farewell with promises of future visits and walked back to Granny's cottage with a happy spring in her step. That was two new friends she had now made. She burst through the door talking excitedly, "Look at the basket I....." Her voice trailed off as she took in the scene before her.

A young man was lying on Granny's cloth-covered kitchen table. He was bleeding heavily from a puncture in his shoulder. It was easy to see what had caused the wound, since the arrow was still protruding from it. Elgin and Granny hovered over the patient and were trying to stem the flow of blood.

"Blast those lazy, good-for-nothing goblins! They would rather work hard to steal from us than forage easy food from the forest. Hang on, Ronan. Granny will mend ye good as new."

Granny noticed Molly standing stock still in the doorway. "Good…ye are here. Grab that kettle, and fill it from the water barrel outside. Set it over the fire, and make sure it boils. Bring those bandages from the shelf....come on, Molly...I need yer help."

Molly gave herself a mental shake and jumped into action. She moved about the room, following Granny's directions. She applied pressure to the wound when directed and helped hold the young man down while Granny pulled the arrow out. The cry of torment that the young man uttered caused Molly's stomach to lurch, but she kept up a steady stream of soothing words to help calm the agonized patient. Soon after, the young man passed out from the pain, and his wound was sterilized and stitched as he lay unconscious. The bleeding slowed and stopped with the application of Granny's healing salves, and everyone breathed a sigh of relief. Elgin brought in a cot and placed it before the fireplace, and the three of them transferred the young man to it for the night. When Granny's kitchen was cleaned and put back in order, they sat down at the table for a cup of herb tea.

"Ye came home just in time, Molly. Ronan had lost a lot of blood, and one more set of hands was sorely needed. Ye did very well. I 'spect ye would make a good healer, and I could use a helper...someone I could teach my craft to," Granny said.

Now that the immediate danger was over and Ronan was sleeping peacefully, Molly's knees were shaking quite badly, and she was glad to be sitting down. Before, her concern for the bleeding patient had taken over, and there had been no time to panic. She stared into her tea mug and after some moments spoke quietly. "My father is a healer, and he is very good at it. He is well known in the city where we live."

It was several minutes before anyone spoke. Elgin was the first to break the silence. "Aye, ye miss him very much...donna ye, Rua?"

Instead of answering, Molly moved into a chair by Ronan and adjusted his covers. While Granny and Elgin talked in muted tones at the table, Molly studied the features of the sleeping young man with dark hair. He was quite tall and his feet hung off the end of the cot. He was also more muscular than Elgin; his age was hard to place. She had not seen him around the village. She supposed that he was part of the group who spent most of their time foraging in the forest for food and supplies.

"We will have to guard the village more closely," Elgin was saying. "The goblins are creating more mischief than usual. They are not usually this brave and certainly not this violent. Something in the forest has changed. I can feel it in the air. I will pass the word that no one leaves the village alone from now on, and we must all carry weapons."

"Have one or two stand guard while the others forage," Granny said.

"Aye...good idea. Is he going to be all right?" he said with a worried look while nodding toward Ronan.

"We've done all that can be done for the moment. My salves should do the trick.....she's got the healing touch...aye, she does," said Granny referring to Molly who was laying a cool cloth on Ronan's brow.

Elgin got to his feet and headed to the door. "I'll be back to check on him on the morrow. Send Molly if ye need me during the night."

Molly volunteered to sit up awhile with Ronan and keep an eye on him. It wouldn't do for him to flay about and rip out his stitches. Granny went to bed, and a few minutes later, soft snores could be heard emanating from her corner of the room. Molly welcomed the chance to sit by the fire and contemplate all that had happened. She was much too keyed up to go directly to sleep anyway. She thought back over the events of the evening, and was rather proud that she had been able to help. She had sprung into action and had followed Granny's directions without questions or hesitation. She had helped save this man's life, and somehow that made her feel very protective toward him. Nothing was going to happen to him on her watch.

She imagined that this was how her father felt when he made his rounds at the hospital. Now she understood why he stayed so late at work and often rushed off when the phone rang summoning him to a patient's bedside. While gazing upon Ronan's sleeping face, the realization dawned on her of how her father must constantly feel torn between his family and his patients. Each demanded so much of his time and attention, and he was amazing at fulfilling everyone's needs.

If I ever make it back home, I am going to hug him fiercely and tell him how wonderful he is.

As Molly rocked quietly beside the sleeping figure, the burning logs shifted in the fireplace sending a shower of sparks up the chimney, and the moon hid its face behind a bank of clouds causing the darkness outside the windows to deepen.

Chapter 9

A soft voice penetrated her consciousness, but it was the tug on her hair that brought her fully awake. She lifted her head and looked about blearily. It took her a moment to realize that she had fallen asleep in the chair and had leaned forward with her head resting on her crossed arms beside Ronan on his cot. The patient, who was now fully awake, had a wan smile on his face.

"Now that is truly the most remarkable eyes I have ever seen," he said softly.

"Thanks. They came with the face," Molly replied with a smile.

As Ronan chuckled quietly, Molly looked about the cottage. Granny still snored softly in her bed as it was very early with dawn barely peeking through the windows. Molly stirred the fire and added another log for warmth and light.

"Could I trouble ye for a glass of water?" he asked. Molly quickly fetched cool water from the rain barrel outside the door and helped him lift his head far enough to drink his fill. He lay back on the pillow with a sigh, and Molly noticed that his face, framed by dark curly hair, was as pale as the pillow beneath his head.

"You're going to be quite weak for a while, but that's to be expected with all the blood you've lost."

"Ye are the Galeing that was rescued from the forest. I heard about ye all the way over in my village. Ye donna look all that scary…why I bet ye have never eaten one child in yer whole life." He uttered this softly with a look of amusement.

"Let me guess…Fenella has appointed herself my press agent, and no, I never eat children without plenty of ketchup handy," she quipped with a wry smile.

His eyebrows shot up while confusion showed on his face. "Aye, I know of Fenella but not this rest agent or Ketchep of whom ye speak. Will I be meeting them soon?"

Molly giggled at his misunderstanding and just shook her head. "So, there are more villages like this one in the forest? I had no idea."

"Aye, there are many other villages and people living in the forest. Our cousins, the fairies, live a half day's walk from here. The gnomes live a day's walk."

"Fairies…gnomes…?" Molly sputtered.

"Aye, they are just forest people like us."

Molly sat staring into the fire trying to wrap her brain around the idea of the forest being populated with so many tiny people….and to think they had been here invisible and undetected for hundreds…or would that be…thousands of years? No one in her world could see them or would believe her if she told them…but then again…as a young child, she had read fairy tale books about elves, hadn't she? Of course, most of the stories were written a hundred years ago and were considered to be fiction. Perhaps, someone long ago from her world had stumbled upon the forest people. Hadn't Granny said that it was rare for a Galeing to be able to see and hear them? Rare and special she had said. Molly didn't feel rare and special. She felt awkward and out of place. She looked nothing like the elves and understood very little about their world.

"Such troubling thoughts for one so young." Ronan's dark eyes had been studying her face for the last few minutes. "I am Ronan from the Misty Falls Village. What are ye called?"

"My name's Molly."

She put her own problems out of her mind and focused on her patient. She felt his forehead and determined that he had no fever. She checked his shoulder wound and saw that the stitches were holding. There were no signs of further bleeding and no streaks of red to indicate infection. Granny's salves must contain an antibiotic of some type. Molly resolved to learn the ingredients of the various salves and poultices that Granny concocted as a healer. She would also pay more attention to the herbs and plants that they harvested from the forest. She was finding the secrets of healing to be very intriguing and had many questions for Granny when she finally awoke.

During all of Molly's tending, Ronan had fallen back asleep, and since he was in no immediate danger, she decided that it was time to get some rest herself. She was asleep as soon as her head hit the pillow.

When she finally opened her eyes, it was close to noon, and Granny was nowhere to be found. Ronan was propped up on enough pillows to put him in a semi-sitting position, and he was eating lunch. His plate and cup were sitting on a wooden chair that served as a table by his bedside. He took in Molly's rumpled appearance with a grin. "About time ye woke up. Is there a bear underneath yer covers? I'm sure I heard one snoring all morning. For such a pretty, little lass ye do make a racket. I threw a shoe at ye and the bear, hoping to stop the noise, but to no avail. Alas, now I am without a shoe and a full night's rest."

Molly responded to his teasing with a wit of her own. With her three brothers, you had to learn to give out as good as you got. "Snoring you say? At least I don't drool. I got up twice during the night to change your pillow and mop up the floor under your bed. The only time you stopped drooling was when you sucked your thumb."

As Molly ducked behind the curtain in the corner to change into a fresh dress, Ronan burst out in loud laughter. "Aaah, Molly May,...ye are a breath of fresh air."

Molly reappeared from behind the curtain and helped herself to some freshly-baked bread and a hunk of cheese. She joined Ronan in front of the stone fireplace, and they munched companionably in silence for a while. "So…does everyone in the forest know of my presence in the village?"

"Aye, word gets passed very quickly from town to town, and a Galeing among us is rousing news indeed."

"How far is your village from here?"

"About a morning's walk in fair weather."

Just then a knock sounded at the door, and Elgin's head appeared. "Looks like ye survived the night, me friend."

Ronan smiled back at Elgin. "Takes more than a goblin arrow to stop me."

"I was talking to Molly Girl, if ye donna mind…..well, did he give ye too much trouble?" This was delivered with Elgin's usual cocky grin. "I hope the village idiot dinna tax yer patience overmuch. Most of the womenfolk handle him by swinging a cooking skillet at his head."

"And brain damage him more than he already is?...I hardly think so," Molly replied. This was just like being home with her brothers. The light exchange of teasing insults warmed her from the inside out. It was obvious that these two had been lifelong friends.

Elgin and Ronan spent several hours visiting while Molly went in search of Granny. She finally found her gathering herbs and roots in the forest on the edge of the village, and they worked together to replenish Granny's store of medicinal plants. While they worked, Granny explained the difference between the plants and their healing qualities. By the time they returned to the cottage, Molly's head was bursting with new information. They found Elgin sitting beside a sleeping Ronan, and they took over his supervision for the rest of the day.

Ronan mended surprisingly fast. Apparently, the forest people had that advantage over the people in Molly's world. The wound healed almost before their eyes, and Ronan recovered his strength and within days no longer slept in Granny's cottage.

A week later, Ronan and Elgin went with Molly into the forest while she gathered herbs, nuts and berries. Everyone in the village was being more cautious in light of the recent trouble with the goblins. The young men kept watch while Molly concentrated on finding the items that Granny had requested. Molly still could not become accustomed to the enormous size of everything outside, and sometimes when she ventured into the woods, she would experience a temporary dizzying sensation.

While she filled her gathering basket, her friends sat on top of a boulder in the sunshine. Ronan pulled out a wooden flute and serenaded them with remarkable talent. The idyllic music added to the splendor of the green forest, and even the birds halted their song to listen. She soon had a full basket and was ready to head back to the village. Elgin was standing beside some hanging vines calling to her. "Come, Molly Girl, let's have a swing."

"Have a swing?" she asked.

"Aye…donna tell me ye have never swung on tree vines." To demonstrate, he stood on a vine that looped down from a tree limb, and Ronan gave him a push. As he glided back and forth through the air, Ronan jumped on a vine and did the same. Molly set down her basket and ran to a likely looking vine and started swinging with abandon. It was quite fun, and it took her back to her childhood when she played on the tire swing under the tree house in the yard of the summer house. By pulling back and then leaning forward, you could swing quite high. She felt lighthearted as she soared through the air and the ground fell away beneath her. Every few minutes one of them would jump from their vine and run to another that looked even better. Ronan and Elgin decided that she should swing much higher, so they positioned themselves in front and behind and pushed her vine with all their might. She laughed as her path of motion climbed to new heights and whooped and hollered in delight as the scenery rushed by.

Molly never saw the rock that came sailing through the air and struck her between the shoulder blades. Suddenly, she became airborne and landed in a pile of moss. She lay stunned for just a moment and then sat up slowly. Her friends were at her side in an instant. When they immediately saw that she was not seriously injured, Elgin stayed by her side while Ronan dashed off into the woods in an attempt to catch the culprit.

"Are ye sure ye are unharmed?" he asked with concern.

"The moss bed broke my fall. I'm fine." She stood up and brushed the leaves and twigs from her dress. Elgin picked some moss from her hair and helped her find her basket at the base of a big sycamore tree. Someone had dumped her basket and scattered the items all around. The berries had been stomped into the grass, but all the other items were easily recovered. By the time they had refilled the basket, Ronan was back and non-too happy. In fact, he was downright livid. "Those goblins have gone too far. They have quite a licking coming. It's time we called a meeting of all the villages," he said in a quiet but hard voice.

As they moved through the forest, Elgin and Ronan walked protectively on each side of Molly and discussed what they would do to the goblins in the future should their paths cross. Since they were already quite agitated and fuming, Molly kept quiet, hoping that they would calm down and not do anything rash. Besides, she wasn't sure goblins were to blame. She had never seen a goblin, and it had all happened so fast. After she had landed on the ground, she thought she had caught a glimpse of someone peeking at them over the top of a boulder…someone with a head of ebony curls.

Chapter 10

When the trio reached the village, Elgin and Ronan walked Molly all the way back to the cottage. After the incident in the woods, they were taking no chances. She deposited the basket on the kitchen table and went in search of Granny. A few minutes later, she found her sitting on a stump behind the house. Granny appeared to be staring up into the treetops.

"What are you doing?" Molly asked.

"Talking to Crionna," Granny replied.

For a moment Molly thought Granny had gone mad, but then she spotted the owl sitting on a branch high up in the tree.

"Do you mean that owl?"

"Aye, she sees many things that occur in the forest and keeps me informed. We have her to thank for finding ye lying under the big tree. She told me where ye were, and she has been guarding ye since the minute ye stepped into the woods."

Molly started to laugh out loud at the silly notion that an owl was able to talk and understand what was going on, but then she remembered where she was. Here, in this world, anything was possible. She sat on the ground and kept quiet as Granny resumed her conversation.

The owl made throaty noises and blinked its eyes at Molly. Granny nodded and spoke in a strange language. The owl responded in its own language and occasionally ruffled its feathers for emphasis. This went on for some time. Then the owl spread its massive wings and flew deeper into the forest. Granny stared after it for several minutes before she slowly got to her feet and headed for the cottage.

She was silent while she set lunch out on the table, and Molly did not press her for information.

When Granny finally spoke, she was quiet and very serious. "The goblins are up to no good, according to Crionna. We haven't had any real trouble with them in quite some time. I'm afraid the balance of the forest has been upset by yer presence in our village, but not to worry....we will face whatever comes." These words seemed ominous to Molly; she tried not to fret. The truth was, though, Granny's words had left her with a strong sense of foreboding.

Molly stayed very busy the next few days as there was always plenty to do in the village. Anyone who went into the forest to gather food or firewood was accompanied by one or more of the men in the village. Word had spread of the attack on Molly. She helped Granny concoct her salves, poultices and potions. Together they gathered herbs, roots, mushrooms and various plants. They hung them to dry from the ceiling of the cottage and then ground them into powder.

Molly was gaining quite an education in the healing arts and assisted Granny whenever patients came by for treatment. On several occasions, Molly watched Thistle's children and helped her around her house, and the two young ladies were becoming close friends with each encounter. The children grew fond of Molly and chattered at her excitedly whenever she came into sight. She learned that Thistle's mate, Hynes, traveled from village to village as a trader and was often gone from home. He had brought back news from the other forest people that the goblins were deviling everyone and that extra caution was being practiced all through the woods.

The people of Hickory Hollow were coming together that evening to discuss the problem of the goblins and other community concerns. Everyone brought food to contribute to the town dinner, and big pots were already simmering in the middle of the settlement. Granny, Molly and the other women laid out food and baked goods on the makeshift tables that the men had earlier set up. Meat was being roasted on a spit over the campfire where the men were gathered. They talked in serious tones as they turned and basted the meat. The village children were captivated by one young man who sat on a log telling stories. Sleeping babies were tucked into woven basket cradles that hung suspended from branches. A warm breeze gently rocked the cradles to and fro and kept the babies happy and content. Molly stirred one of the big pots of bubbling stew that was sitting on a fire and listened to the women's friendly chatter. When she felt a tug at her skirt, she looked down to discover Thistle's toddler son peering up at her.

"Where did you come from, you little rascal?" She picked him up and set him on her hip and resumed stirring the pot. The wee one laid his head on Molly's shoulder and promptly went to sleep.

"Ye look as if ye've been a part of this village all yer life," a quiet voice said. Molly turned and found Elgin leaning against the trunk of a tree.

"How long have you been standing there?"

"Long enough to see that Thistle's babes have taken quite a liking to ye."

Molly turned back to the pot she was stirring so that Elgin did not see her blush in embarrassment. It was true that she was gaining more acceptance from the villagers, and every day she was feeling more comfortable in this world.

"This one is getting heavier by the minute. Let's go find Thistle," Molly said. She and Elgin found the baby's mother in just a few minutes, and he was put down on a pallet to finish his nap. They both returned to the cooking fire, and Molly resumed her stirring.

"Where is Ronan today? It's unusual to see one of you without the other....kind of like a two-headed goblin," Molly teased.

"Ronan had to return to Misty Falls Village for a few days, but he'll be back. Are ye missing that ugly mug of his, Molly Girl?"

"Like I'd miss a toothache," she retorted with a sideways grin.

Soon, the food was ready, and everyone milled around, helping themselves to the appetizing feast. Molly found herself ladling up the stew, and to her surprise, Fenella was the first one in line. Fenella took her full bowl without comment and walked away.

Well....maybe I really am finally becoming accepted.

Unfortunately, her feelings of relief were short lived. Fenella was gagging and spitting food out on the ground and causing quite a commotion.

"Stop! Donna eat the stew! She is trying to poison us!" Fenella was now screeching loudly in a hateful manner. The villagers froze with spoons halfway to their mouths. They stared at their bowls and then at Molly who was still standing by the big pot, too shocked to respond. Granny hurried over, grabbed a big spoon and took a tentative sip. She quickly spit it out and instructed everyone to discard the contents of their bowls.

"Bitter herbs have been added that will make ye very sick if ye eat it," she informed the crowd. "They must have been added by mistake, but we've caught it in time, and no harm has been done."

Fenella sputtered and pointed an accusing finger toward Molly. "There's been a mistake all right! It's a mistake to bring a Galeing into our midst and welcome her into our homes. When will all of ye see that?" She glared at Molly for several seconds and then looked about her for support from the villagers.

"Who else helped with the stew?" someone asked.

Elgin answered in a quiet voice, "Anyone could have put those herbs in the pot when Molly and I went in search of Thistle. Molly would not harm us. I trust her with my life."

"Aye, and I trust her with my children," said Thistle stepping forward.

As Molly looked into the faces of the villagers, she could see their indecision. They did not know whom to believe. If she was in their place, she would not trust an outsider either. She really could not blame them.

The stew was discarded, and the feasting resumed but with a more serious and subdued atmosphere. Molly fixed her plate and then found a place to sit on the outside edge of the crowd...where she felt she belonged. Elgin took a seat beside her.

"Donna worry yer head none, Molly Girl. The truth will out....ye will see"

But Molly did worry. In her world, she had never been unjustly accused of such contemptible actions, and it gnawed at her very core. She had a good idea of who had tampered with the stew.

"Why would Fenella do such a thing? Why does she hate me so much? She would chance making everyone in the village sick to get at me?" Molly asked this in a miserable voice with downcast eyes.

Elgin shrugged and sighed heavily. "I suppose she is threatened by a pretty girl who arrived under mysterious circumstances and who has captured the attention and interest of the villagers. Since we've found ye in the woods, all the villages have talked of little else. Ye have become quite famous."

Molly looked at him in surprise. Pretty? Mysterious? Famous? She had no idea that she was regarded in that fashion. She could not quite wrap her head around this astonishing concept. Back home she was just an ordinary girl who was ignored by the boys in school. Her mother constantly berated her for various shortcomings, and her brothers treated her like a favorite pet...never taking her seriously.

Since she had stepped into the woods, everything had changed. Sometimes the changes sent her reeling. If her family and friends could see her now, what would they think? Here she was...sitting at the base of an enormous hickory tree wearing a pale blue homespun dress and handmade soft leather shoes. Her only adornment was a blue ribbon tied in her hair. Her companion was a tall, slim, young man with exotic, striking features and shoulder length, brown hair tied back at the nape of his neck. He looked like something that had stepped out of the pages of a fantasy novel, and Molly was once again overcome with feelings of surrealism.

The villagers, finished with their meal, were discussing the present goblin situation. There seemed to be no formal town council. Everyone in the village had equal standing, and all took their turns speaking.

"The goblins haven't been such trouble in the past...mischievous and thieving to be sure, but they are becoming dangerous," Bantry, the furniture maker, was saying.

"I heard one of the fairies was worked over mighty well by three of them. He finally perched on a tree limb out of reach while the goblins threw rocks, and eventually, some of his friends came and chased them away," said another villager. "He was lucky to escape with just bumps and bruises."

"Aye...Ronan 'twasn't so lucky," another replied, and there were murmurs of agreement all around.

"What about the child the goblins tried to steal in Willow Grove Village? They've never threatened our children before," said Thistle. "This is worrisome, indeed!"

"Maybe we should arrange a surprise attack and give them a taste of their own medicine!" a voice said from the crowd.

The discussion went on for some time. It was ultimately decided that only groups of five or more should go into the forest and that at least two men would carry weapons and stand guard at all times. It was late when the meeting broke up. Everyone's face carried a worried expression as they headed back to their homes for the night.

Elgin walked Granny and Molly to their door and saw them safely inside before he said goodnight. The ladies prepared for bed and climbed gratefully into their perspective bunks. It had been a day of excitement and not all of it welcome. Although she was tired, Molly had a hard time going to sleep right away. She gazed out the window at the moon peeking through the tree limbs.

It was some time later before her breathing finally slowed and she closed her eyes in slumber. In her dreams, Fenella and the goblins chased each other through the forest cackling madly while she sat high in a tree and watched them from above. An owl sitting on the limb beside her blinked knowingly and then transformed into Granny and flew away. Molly turned restlessly in her sleep and mumbled incoherently as the moon slowly followed its age-old path across the dark sky.

Chapter 11

A few days later, a large group of women planned to pick berries and gather nuts in the forest. Granny had encouraged Molly to join the outing, so she packed a lunch and headed to the center of town. She carried a new basket in each hand and was quite proud of the vessels that she herself had woven. The day promised to be bright and sunny, and there was an energetic spring to her step. Her enthusiasm faded abruptly when she saw that Fenella would be going also, but she squared her shoulders and decided that Miss Ravenhair would not ruin her day. *Just let her try to start something with me. I will snatch all that pretty hair out of her head.*

As the group of 15 or so ladies set out into the forest with their armed guards, Molly made it a point to avoid Fenella. She needn't to have bothered, though, because Fenella kept her distance and totally ignored her. Soon, she forgot all about being wary of Fenella as she became engrossed in the excited chatter of the other women.

As they filled their baskets with huckleberries, the women gossiped and exchanged stories of their husbands and children. They swapped recipes for favorite dishes and home cures and talked about knitting patterns and colicky babies. Molly did not join in the conversations but hovered on the fringe, listening to it all. She really had nothing to add, and after the stew fiasco, she supposed it was better to not draw attention to herself.

The most exciting topic of discussion was the upcoming Gathering of all the forest villages in a few weeks. The Gathering took place once every three years, and it was being held this year in Misty Falls Village. That was the reason for the massive berry picking and nut collecting that was going on today. The ladies would make pastries, jams, jellies and candies to take to the three-day festival.

The Gathering was part celebration, part swap meet and part family reunion to which everyone would bring items to trade and barter. It was also a chance to visit distant relatives and friends. Many of the ladies had met their future husbands at past Gatherings and related the details to the younger women who had yet to be married.

As Molly listened to the stories, she realized that the forest people mated for life. There was no talk of divorce or separation that was so common in her world. Marriages lasted a lifetime here. She also realized that they regarded their offspring as precious beings. That was a far cry from her world where so many of her classmates did not even live with both parents. Most lived with a single parent or in blended families that included a step-parent and their children. Many others had been totally abandoned by both parents and were being raised by a relative or a complete stranger.

If only my world could be a bit more like this place.

At noon, the ladies and their guards sat in the shade and ate from their lunch baskets. Molly wished that Thistle had come along today so that she would have someone to chat with, but apparently, she didn't have anyone to look after the children. One or two of the women had brought their wee ones on the berry-picking trip. They had strapped the babies on their backs in cloth carriers, leaving their hands free to work. The babies mostly slept and rarely cried. It amazed Molly that the mothers in the village could take care of their babies easily without all the commercial items that were sold in stores back home.

After lunch, the ladies returned to gathering nuts and picking berries. Some of the women wanted to find the wild blueberries that grew in the forest, so they headed to another part of the woods with two of the guards going along for protection. Molly stayed behind with the other group and continued to fill her baskets. The women fanned out to find the best berries and nuts, and their voices soon faded to a quiet hum as they moved a few yards away. Molly became lost in her own thoughts as she searched for the plants that were heavy with fat berries.

By her calculations, she had been in Hickory Hollow for six weeks now. She wondered for the hundredth time what her family must think of her disappearance. Did her mother miss her at all? She knew her brothers and her father would be out of their minds with worry, but would her mother really care? Or would she feel a sense of relief? At an early age, Molly had realized that she was the child her mother hadn't wanted. She had spent years trying to gain her mother's favor only to fail time and time again. Her mother might love her out of a sense of duty, but she simply did not like her. At best, she tolerated her. The rest of the family was blind to these cold, hard facts. Her mother covered her feelings well when they were present but didn't bother when they weren't. That was when Molly was subjected to her mother's outright resentment or, even worse, her cold indifference. She had shed many tears over this situation but had never been able to determine how to win her mother's acceptance.

Yet, Granny, on the other hand, had taken her in and had cared for her as if she were her own. In fact, the two women had become very close and had formed a bond as if they were mother and daughter. Granny had never criticized or rebuked her harshly for mistakes made and had become very proud of Molly as she had learned the secrets of the art of healing. Just lately, she had shown her confidence in Molly by turning over the care of several patients with minor injuries who had presented themselves at their cottage door. Her father and brothers loved her unconditionally, and now a complete stranger had found her worthy of love and trust.

If I ever make it back home, I will find some way to bridge the distance between my mother and myself.

Lost in her own thoughts for some time, Molly hadn't noticed that the other women's voices had completely faded. She called out some of their names but to no avail. She was completely alone in the small clearing. She walked first one way and then the other, straining to hear their voices but never losing sight of the clearing. When leaving the village, she had paid little attention to which direction they had walked to reach the berry patch, and now she had no earthly idea how to get back. The irony of the situation was not lost on her, however.

Is there some kind of award given for constantly becoming lost in this forest? I seem to have a real talent for it.

There was nothing to do but sit and wait. Surely someone would notice her missing and come looking for her. It was best not to wander from the berry patch, since this would be one of the first places they would look. She set her full baskets down at the base of a large tree and dropping down beside them, resigned herself to waiting.

She leaned back against the trunk and hummed softly to occupy her time. Within minutes, she had slipped into a light slumber unaware of the time that passed. The next time she opened her eyes, the shadows in the clearing had lengthened considerably, but Molly took no notice. She was wide awake now and feeling the cold, icy grip of full blown terror. With her heart pounding frantically, she looked into the face of the ugliest, most horrendous creature she had ever seen.

Chapter 12

The creature had thrust his face into hers and was staring intently. Molly was holding her breath...too shocked and frightened to move. It had gray skin covered in warts, a long nose that curved down toward the chin, sharp yellow teeth and breath that reeked of decay. She shrank back against the tree as it tilted its head to one side and peered at her even more intently. It uttered something in a strange language, and two more of the creatures emerged from the bushes. With the tree at her back and these creatures in front of her, Molly had no path of escape.

Goblins!

They stood staring at her muttering to each other for several minutes. It was obvious that she was their topic of conversation. She took this chance to size them up. They were about her height, not especially muscular, but possessing sharp claws that appeared to be dangerous. Their heads and feet were the biggest part of their bodies which were thin and wiry. Even though they wore rags of some kind, their scant clothing gave no indication if they were male or female.

As she observed them, she tried to remain calm and think. At one point she could have sworn they said something to the effect of...."We have found her," but she couldn't be sure. If she was going to have any chance to get away, she would have to use the element of surprise. *Let them think I am meek and helpless.*

Just then, two of the goblins grabbed her by the arms and hauled her to her feet. They began walking through the forest taking Molly with them. After several minutes of walking, Molly had offered no resistance, so one of the goblins let go of her arm. She walked a little further letting her compliance lull them into a false sense of security before she made her move.

With no warning, she whirled abruptly and savagely drove the base of her palm into the goblin's nose. Everything her brothers had taught her about self-defense came back in a flash. She silently prayed that goblins had the same pressure points as Galeings so that her plan would be successful.

It worked!

The goblin released her arm and fell to the ground howling in pain. Before the other two could react, she had bolted into the woods. She ran like a deer, fleeing from a pack of lions and never heard the footsteps behind her. She flew through bushes and dodged trees and low-hanging limbs. She abruptly came to a rude halt when one of the goblins grabbed a handful of her hair, and she was slammed to the ground. She landed with her hand on a large stick, so she was on her feet in an instant swinging it with all her might.

She caught the ugly creature alongside the head and laid him out on the ground as the second goblin emerged from the bushes. She rounded on him next, and he got a blow to the stomach for his troubles. While he was doubled over trying to catch his breath, the third goblin came out from behind a tree and advanced in a cautious crouch. This one had learned his lesson already as his bright red nose and streaming eyes attested to the fact. Molly decided that a show of aggressiveness would be the best strategy. She started determinedly toward the goblin thrusting with the stick.

"Come on, you stinky breath, scum sucking, maggot faced, sorry excuse for a goblin. I'm going to whip you like I'm your momma and send you home crying." She had stared directly into the goblin's face, and her voice was hard as steel as she delivered her threat.

Her demeanor had the desired effect that she hoped, and the goblin looked confused as he slowly began to retreat. With just a few steps, he had backed himself into a large tree trunk and was starting to look panicked. SHWANG! An arrow flew through the air and pinned the top part of his ear to the tree. While Molly worked the pinned goblin over with her stick, the other two took off into the forest, dodging arrows as they ran. The trapped goblin finally yanked free of the arrow and took off, leaving a small part of his ear behind.

Still locked into survival mode, Molly whirled around fiercely swinging the stick at the figures that had come up behind her. Elgin and Ronan jumped back just in time, throwing up hands that held their bows in surrender.

"Take it easy, Molly Girl," Elgin said softly. "It's just us."

Molly stood panting from exertion and slowly lowered the stick as Elgin stepped forward to take it from her. The adrenaline rush was still racing in her system; she just stood and looked at them blankly. Ronan put his arms around her and said, "Relax...ye are safe. Remind me never to make ye mad."

Molly leaned her forehead on his chest, laughed weakly and sent up a silent prayer of gratitude. *Thank you, God, for three older brothers who taught me how to defend myself.*

"How did you know to come looking for me?" she asked.

"No one realized ye were missing until the berry pickers returned to the village. Each group thought ye were with the other until Granny noticed yer absence. In fact, someone insisted they had seen ye with one of the groups coming back," Ronan answered.

Molly and Elgin both looked directly at each other and said, "Fenella!" in unison. Ronan looked confused, "Ye will have to catch me up later. I think we should get out of the woods before night falls."

"Agreed," said Elgin. The young men searched the surrounding area and retrieved as many arrows as they could find and then hustled Molly back toward the village. Along the way, Elgin filled Ronan in on the details of the village dinner and their suspicions about Fenella's involvement in ruining the stew. Now that Molly had seen the goblins up close, she was sure that Fenella had been behind the rock-throwing incident also, and she shared that information with her friends. Looking up at their faces, she could see that they were infuriated, and, for once, she felt a little sorry for Fenella.

By the time they reached the edge of the village, the young men had formed a plan. They hid Molly behind one of the cottages and instructed her not to come out until she was called. From her hiding place, she would be able to hear all that was said.

Elgin and Ronan sprinted into the middle of town where a crowd was gathered. "Is Molly here?" they asked. The crowd milled about excitedly with everyone talking at once. The young men looked distressed and sorrowful.

"This was the only thing we found," and they produced a scrap of fabric that they had torn from the hem of her dress. "This was caught in a bush by her gathering baskets that were left sitting under a tree," said Elgin. "Almost anything could have happened to her. How could ye leave her in the woods all alone?"

One especially upset young woman answered, "But we dinna know. We were told that she was with the other group."

Another one spoke up, "And we were told that she was with yer group!"

"Who told ye this?" Ronan asked quietly.

"Fenella!" they both replied. The crowd parted to reveal a red-faced Fenella in the middle of the villagers.

"I don't think that's really what I said…," she stammered. She looked about for a way to escape but the villagers had closed ranks around her. They stood silently, staring in contempt. "Ye have twisted my words…I'm sure she's fine…" she continued to make excuses.

"If the goblins dinna get her, then a fox or a wolf has picked up her scent by now. We'll never find her," Ronan said in a voice just above a whisper. Thistle uttered a small cry of anguish while all the blood drained from Fenella's face.

"But I dinna mean to….I only wanted to play a trick…" she said looking about for support in the villagers' faces but finding none.

"Who threw the rock that knocked her out of the swing that day in the forest?" asked Elgin.

"And who tampered with the stew?" asked Ronan

The guilt on Fenella's face was answer enough. Everyone could immediately see exactly what had taken place.

"Molly, I think the rat has caught itself in the trap. Ye can come on out now," said Ronan.

As Molly emerged from behind the cottage, she was surrounded by excited villagers asking questions all at once. Fenella stared in shock for a few moments. Once she realized the crowd's attention was no longer on her, she made good her escape and slinked away.

Molly found Granny in the crowd, grabbing her in an enormous hug. “I'm sorry we had to pretend that I was still missing, but it was the only way to get to the truth.”

Granny hugged her back and said, “Donna fret, dearie. Crionna beat ye back to the village and told me all that happened with the goblins. Are ye sure ye are unharmed?”

Ronan, who had overheard the conversation, spoke up in a loud voice that carried over the noise of the crowd…a crowd that had grown since the word had gone out of Molly's return. “Unharmed, ye say? She's fine…but ye canna be saying that about the goblins. They'll be limping home tonight sore and bruised from the beating she gave them.”

Molly blushed when all eyes turned on her in surprise. “I don't think I would have made it if it hadn't been for Elgin and Ronan turning up when they did. They saved me.”

“Molly May, ye were trouncing those goblins all on yer own. I'm just glad we showed up in time to see it!” said Ronan.

Molly's friends told the story of her fight with the goblins to the wide-eyed crowd who hung on their every word. Molly tried to correct them when they exaggerated, but it was no use.

She had learned that the villagers appreciated a good yarn better than anything. She gave up trying to keep the story accurate and discreetly backed her way to the edge of the crowd. She received pats on the back, hugs and well wishes as she went through the villagers. She located Granny, and they headed home as the night settled around them.

Laughter could be heard from the middle of town where a campfire had been lit and a barrel tapped. As the moon rose high in the sky, the crickets started their evening chorus and it was some time later before the whole village was abed and sleeping soundly.

Chapter 13

The next morning found Molly and Granny having breakfast at the kitchen table. Molly was grateful for the peace and quiet after yesterday's traumatic adventure. She sipped her tea and wondered about the goblin's strange statement that he had found her. Had they been looking for her? How did they know who she was? If they were mainly thieves, why hadn't they just taken her full baskets and left? Where had they planned to take her?

Granny watched Molly's face as she pondered these questions.

"Well…out with it, child. What troubling thoughts are weighing heavy on yer mind?" she asked.

It's something the goblins said yesterday. I could have sworn that one told the others that they had found me. It's probably nothing....it just struck me as strange."

"Is there anything else they said?"

"They talked among themselves about me, but I couldn't make it out."

"Something is brewing with the goblins. I'll have to look further into the situation."

"Will Crionna know what's going on?"

"Aye...she's not the only one I'll be talking with...many other forest creatures will have seen or heard something. Even the trees will be whispering. It's just a matter of knowing how to listen."

Suddenly it struck Molly how absurd all this would be in her world. She was sitting in a forest village talking to an ancient elf who conversed with trees and owls about her fight with goblins. Here, though, such things were ordinary occurrences....well, not completely...the goblins had stepped up their aggressiveness all over the forest, and all the villages were alarmed. She had no desire to meet those ugly goblins face-to-face again anytime soon.

"I am told Fenella left the village this morning," Granny said.

"Where did she go?"

"It seems Elgin and Ronan volunteered to escort her to Misty Falls Village, so she packed her bags and left at daylight. She most likely will stay with her kin there for quite some time. She won't be bothering ye anymore. Hopefully, she has learned her lesson."

Either that or I now have an enemy for life.

As the morning wore on, Molly left the cottage to pay a visit to Thistle and her children. As she made her way through the village, town folks spoke and greeted her with much enthusiasm. Several of them had never addressed her before, and she was encouraged that her standing as an intruder had been elevated to trusted friend.

"Is that apple pie I smell?" she asked when Thistle answered her knock.

"Yer just in time. I just pulled it from the oven. The apple trees around the village put out a good crop this year. There will be plenty of apple mead for the town and for trading."

After the two ladies enjoyed a slice of pie, they both got busy with other tasks. Molly began making more baskets to replace the ones she had left in the forest. She also played with the children and kept them occupied while Thistle hand stitched a colorful quilt that she planned to take and trade at the upcoming Gathering. Molly was curious about Fenella's hasty departure and thought Thistle might know the particulars.

"I've heard that Fenella is on her way to Misty Falls Village.....did Elgin and Ronan force Fenella to leave?" she asked.

Thistle's hands hesitated in her sewing for a few seconds. "Let's just say that she was strongly encouraged by most of the village to pay a visit to kinfolk," Thistle said without looking up.

"Will she be allowed to return?"

"She will have to redeem herself in some way if she wishes to become a part of the town again. As it stands, she has disgraced herself with her cruel behavior toward ye. Our rules are few and easily followed, but what she had done is intolerable. So, she has been banished to another village. If she continues to behave in such a manner, all the villages will banish her, and she will be no longer be welcome anywhere."

"If that happens, where will she go? How will she live?"

"She will be sent into the forest to make her own way as best she can. Maybe the goblins would take her in..."

Molly shivered involuntarily. "I wouldn't wish that on anyone."

Thistle shrugged, "Fenella has always been stubborn and headstrong and makes her own choices....now maybe her ill will toward ye has faded a bit."

Changing the subject, Molly asked, "Is the Gathering as much fun as it sounds?"

"Aye, for sure...tis a fine time. Ronan's village is set beside lovely waterfalls, and all the forest people are looking forward to a rousing good time. There'll be lots of music and dancing. There's a storytelling contest...Bantry has won that many times in the past. Lots of bartering and swapping of goods. The fairy people weave the most beautiful cloth from spider silk...I'm hoping to make a trade for some to bring back. Hynes knows all the best items available since he travels to all the villages. Yer baskets would make a good trade....not everyone has ye gifted hands. Weave some for the Gathering, and do a bit of trading while ye are there."

"Do you think the other forest people will think me strange?"

"When they see how we all accept ye, there should be no problems. I'm sure Ronan has talked about ye to his townsfolk, and that will smooth the way, donna ye know." She grew quiet and thoughtful for several minutes before she spoke again. "I've noticed the way Ronan looks at ye…I've never seen him look at any other girl that way."

As Molly started weaving a new basket, she frowned in response. "I'm sure you're mistaken. He and Elgin are both my friends....and soon I will be going home. I don't belong here, Thistle. Even if I could stay, I'm not sure I would choose to. I miss my family terribly, and I have a life waiting for me in my world."

"I've been meaning to ask…what 'tis it like in the Galeing world?"

Molly thought for several seconds before answering. *How do I explain a place so vastly different than this?*

"Our towns are larger, and there's a lot more people scurrying about."

"Where might they be going in such a hurry?"

"They have jobs that take them away from home and…well…." Molly's voice halted as she struggled to find the words. *What is so important back home that keeps us running around?*

"Do ye have a job, as well?"

"I help take care of other people's children sometimes, but I still live at home with my parents. Very soon, though, I will leave home like my brothers and study for a career."

"What is this…career?"

"A way to make a living….so I can live independently and not rely on my parents anymore."

"And do ye have a young fella waiting for ye back home?"

"No…maybe someday I will meet the right man and have a family, but I'm not ready for that just yet…" Molly shrugged. "At least we don't have ugly goblins where I come from. Although…I have seen some pretty homely guys at my high school."

Thistle laughed appreciatively, "But I bet none so fair of face as Ronan…eh?"

Molly flashed her a small smile, and in the most nonchalant voice she could muster, she said, "He is one handsome man, and there is certainly no guy in my school that comes close to being that attractive."

Because Molly was looking down at the basket she was assembling in her lap, she missed the self-satisfied look on her friend's face. Their talk circled back once again to the subject of the Gathering, and the hours passed quickly. It was late afternoon when she took her leave and not before hugs and kisses had been doled out to the small children who had become quite attached to Molly and responded to her departure with wails of disappointment.

As she strolled through the village in the gathering dusk, she wondered if her future would include a husband and children. She began picturing herself in a white wedding gown, walking down a petal-strewn aisle on the arm of her father while soft music played. A tall man waited at the front of the church amid flowers and lit candles. As she drew near, he turned with a smile, and she found herself looking up into the face of …Ronan. Shock caused her to abruptly end the daydream as she gave herself a mental shake.

What are you thinking? He may be the best-looking guy who's ever noticed you're alive, Molly, but he's not for you. Put him out of your head once and for all.

And with that, she continued on to Granny's house which was now in sight. Its windows glowed with welcoming, yellow light, and the smoke coming from the chimney told of a cheery fire blazing on the hearth filling the cottage with warmth.

Chapter 14

One bright morning, Granny announced that she was going to run errands about the village. She donned her shawl and hung a basket on her arm, declaring that she would be back soon and then hustled out the door. Molly looked around the small dwelling and decided to do some cleaning to keep busy. She tied a cloth around her hair and tackled the job at hand. An hour later, she had disposed of the cold fireplace ashes, had swept the hearth, brought in a supply of wood and stacked it in its place by the wall, made the beds and swept the cottage floor clean. She then spied a high shelf holding various clay containers and remembered that Granny had once remarked that it needed a good dusting, so she placed a kitchen chair against the wall and climbed onto the seat.

Just as she began moving the crockery to dust the shelf, she felt the chair give way. One of the chair legs broke with a loud crack, and as Molly began to fall, she clutched the shelf for support. The shelf was ripped from the wall, and clay pots went flying through the air as she landed on the cottage floor. Thankfully, she was not hurt, but as she sat up and surveyed the damage, she felt her heart sink. In just a few short minutes, she had managed to destroy a chair, a shelf and numerous dishes and containers.

Just then, the door to the cottage opened and Granny stood in the entrance with a look of dismay on her face. She dropped her basket and rushed to Molly's side. "Child, are ye hurt?"

As Molly began apologizing profusely, she realized that tears were streaming down her face. "I will clean up the mess…I am so sorry, Granny…I fell while trying to clean the high shelf…" Her voice trailed off in a panic while she gestured at the broken clay pieces scattered across the floor. Meanwhile, Granny had begun an examination of Molly's limbs looking for bumps, bruises or broken bones. Seeing none, she sat back on her heels and said, "Ye donna seem to be seriously hurt, so why the tears?"

"I thought you were upset when you saw everything I destroyed…"

"I was upset that ye might have hurt yerself terribly, and I confess…my heart skipped a beat or two when I saw ye on the floor. The rest is easily repaired and replaced, but ye are not, dear lassie."

As the two ladies got to their feet, Molly managed to step on the hem of her dress and the sound of ripping cloth was heard. Looking down she saw a large rent, and her tears flowed anew. "I am so sorry…so sorry…," she sobbed.

Granny drew her down to sit on the kitchen bench and hugged her tight. "Molly, my dear…there's no need to cry. Hush…hush...now, Rua."

Molly drew back and looked up into the older woman's face. "You're not angry about the broken chair…the shelf…the smashed dishes?" she asked in amazement.

"Good heavens…why would ye think I would be in a temper about that?"

Molly dropped her eyes down to her hands in her lap. "My mother would have been furious at just one of those mishaps…I can only imagine how awful she would have reacted to all of this."

Molly took a shuddering breath and poured her heart out to Granny. It was like a dam had burst as she held nothing back. She spoke of her mother's cold disdain and how for years she had attempted to do something…anything to win her mother's approval. She revealed the pain she felt every time her mother showed pride in Molly's brothers' accomplishments but criticized her own successes. As far back as she could remember, she had never done anything that put a smile on her mother's face. According to her, Molly didn't talk right, walk right…or even breathe correctly. When she had completely bared her soul and the words had run out, she fell silent.

Granny, too, was quiet for several minutes before she finally spoke. "Do ye think, dear lassie, that maybe ye are not at fault here? I believe that yer mother is the one who is lacking. For whatever reason, her heart is crippled, and we may never know why. What I do know is that ye are not to blame for her failings."

Granny took Molly's face in both hands forcing her to look into her eyes. "Do ye know how happy I have been since ye have arrived in our village? I wished for a mate and a houseful of children, but it was never to be. Ye are the daughter that I longed for all these years, and I would never let anyone speak against ye."

Molly responded to the kind words by throwing her arms around Granny and hugging her with all her might. Her heart filled with joy to have found a mother who truly loved her just as she was. She did not see the tears that gathered in Granny's eyes as her hug was warmly returned in kind.

"Well…I think we should sweep up and have ourselves a spot o' tea. This has been quite a morning," said Granny.

Soon, Molly had the floor cleaned of debris and had changed dresses. While Granny was putting the kettle on, a knock sounded at the door. Before either one could answer it, Elgin stuck his head in and grinned broadly.

"Ronan and I are going fishing and thought Molly might like to come."

"'Tis a fine idea, Elgin. She needs to be outside enjoying this beautiful day."

"But I need to help you with the shelf…," Molly protested.

"There is nothing ye can do…Bantry will come 'round and fix the shelf and put a new leg on the chair…off with ye now while the fish are biting."

That was all Elgin needed to hear as he grabbed Molly by the hand and pulled her out the door. "Are ye daft, girl? Why would ye want to stay in on a day like today? Have ye never been fishing?"

"I've been fishing plenty with my brothers. The real question is…do you and Ronan mind being shown up by a girl?"

Elgin laughed as they headed out of the village. Ronan was waiting on the edge of town with the fishing equipment and broke into a happy grin when he saw Molly accompanying Elgin.

"Molly May, so good of ye to join us. We were wondering what to use for bait, and now that we have ye, we can just tie a rope around ye middle and toss ye in the stream," said Ronan with his dark eyes twinkling.

"You won't be so happy when I catch more fish than the village simpletons and put you to shame," she replied.

They loaded their arms with the fishing equipment and headed for the nearest stream. Using supple sticks with string tied on the end for fishing rods, they fastened pungent hunks of cheese on the hooks and cast them into the slow-moving water. With the sunshine flitting between the leaves and the mild temperature, it was the perfect day for fishing as the three friends sat on the bank of the brook. Within minutes, they began catching good-sized fish that Elgin took off the hook and dropped into the reed basket they had brought and tied to a branch to lower into the edge of the water.

They indulged in friendly banter as they kept count of who was catching the most fish, and the competition added to an already enjoyable outing. "That makes six each for me and Molly. Ye only have three, me friend. Why donna ye quit now as to save yerself from embarrassment? We will keep quiet around the village about how yer ugly features scared the fish away from yer hook," teased Elgin while casting a wink in Molly's direction.

"Quiet?...since when have ye ever been quiet? Yer endless yapping is what is driving the fish away right now," answered Ronan.

While Molly was giggling at their jesting, something large and powerful yanked the fishing pole right out of her hands. She scrambled on her hands and knees to overtake the pole as it was being dragged along the bank. In unison, Elgin and Ronan hollered, "NO, MOLLY…LET IT GO!", but her hands were already closing around the pole and she regained her footing. As she turned to smile reassuringly at the boys, she was jerked off her feet.

Chapter 15

While Molly was being dragged facedown along the river bank, it never occurred to her to release the fishing pole. In fact, she had a death grip on the stick and was fighting to halt the forward movement. The line went slack just as the boys reached her, and she sat up with a look of triumph. Whatever had taken the hook decided to try to escape again and yanked her forward toward the water. This time, the boys grabbed her by the ankles or she would have gone in head first.

"JUST LET GO, MOLLY!" Ronan sounded panicked.

"No way!" she shot back.

The tug of war continued with strong yanks that almost pulled her arms out of their sockets. As the tugs inched her forward, the boys would pull her back while trying to convince her to let go of the pole. At one point, when she was almost in the water, Ronan and Elgin dug in their heels and gave a mighty yank, and the string on the fishing pole snapped, sending them both reeling backwards.

Sitting up slowly, Molly was feeling disappointed until she caught the looks on the boys' faces.

"Why dinna ye let go…what were ye tryin' to do?" asked Elgin.

"A good fisherman never loses his pole in the water…my brothers taught me that…what?...," she broke off when she saw the two young men exchanging glances and shaking their heads.

"Did ye stop to think what was on the hook that was so vast and strong? A fish that size would have swallowed ye once he pulled ye in the water," Ronan said exasperatedly.

Molly's face turned white as a sheet as the realization dawned. How could she be so dumb? She had been caught up in the excitement of landing a big catch, and the thought of showing up the boys had caused her to forget where she was. All of a sudden, she felt light headed, and she flopped back on the grass.

The boys rushed to her side and peered down into her face.

"Are ye alright?" Elgin asked.

"I think we scared the wits out of her," Ronan said.

"I'm okay…I just feel really stupid…and a little scared," she admitted.

After a few minutes, her panic attack passed, and she was able to get to her feet. The boys retrieved the basket of fish from the stream along with the fishing gear, and the threesome headed down the short path that led to town. Absorbed in somber thoughts about Molly's close call, for once, Elgin and Ronan did not have much to say.

Finally, Molly broke the silence. "Well, I guess we will both have quite a story to tell tonight about the one that got away."

"Both?" Elgin asked quizzically with raised eyebrows.

"Yep…me **and** the fish."

With that, both young men roared with laughter all the way back to the village.

The next week passed uneventfully, and the time of the Gathering approached quickly. One afternoon Granny and Molly packed a pull cart with items that they would need on the trip, and the next morning Granny began making a special concoction using various herbs and plants. "We donna want those goblins thinking they can come in the village to plunder and steal while we are all away," she said. "Ye and I will be the last to leave for the gathering, and we'll cast a protection spell over the town."

Granny worked on the mixture for an hour before announcing it was ready. By then, the village was virtually empty....except for Molly, Granny and two of the village men who would be their escorts through the forest. Molly carried a bucket while Granny dribbled the magic potion onto the ground with a ladle. They made an entire circle around the village, and then Granny pronounced them finished and ready to leave.

The men took charge of the wooden pull cart while Granny and Molly strapped bundles onto their backs for the trip. Molly paused at the edge of town and looked back. "Is your potion really going to protect the village while we're gone?" she asked worriedly.

The two men exchanged amused glances at her skepticism. “Try stepping back into the village and see what happens,” Granny said.

Molly took several steps back in the opposite direction. As soon as she stepped across the liquid on the ground, she found herself outside the potion circle and feeling a little dazed and confused. She tried once more to cross the line, but it happened again. She could not get past the circle that she and Granny had made with the brew. “What happened?”

Granny chuckled in amusement. “That’s the magic, dearie. Come on...we have quite a walk ahead of us.”

The path to Misty Falls Village appeared to be often used and looked easy to follow. Molly was apprehensive about Granny’s ability to walk the far distance, but she soon realized that she needn’t be. Granny might appear to be elderly and feeble, but she had the strength and stamina of a much younger person. The four travelers passed through bright meadows now and then but mostly walked in the shade of the towering hardwood trees. Birds sang sweetly in the foliage high overhead, and the excited chatter of squirrels could be heard from time to time. It was a pleasant journey through the woods, and the group stopped for a short time beside a rushing stream for lunch. They completed the trip without any mishaps or attacks from the goblins for which everyone breathed a sigh of relief.

Molly was captivated by the final stretch of the trail that was lined with trees in full blossom. As the air was stirred by breezes, pink petals floated down like snowflakes. The travelers rounded the last curve and paused as the breathtaking village came into view. Ronan’s village was positioned beside a swift stream that wound around the town and disappeared into the forest. Beyond the village, a picturesque waterfall produced a mist so fine at the base that the falling water disappeared into a cloud.

Granny, watching Molly’s face, nodded with understanding. “It still takes my breath away, and I have seen it many times in many seasons.”

Molly was at a loss for words in the presence of such an enchanting sight. She just stood with eyes wide and took it all in. After a few minutes, the four travelers headed for the wooden bridge that spanned the stream and led to the village.

Chapter 16

The people of Hickory Hollow had set up an encampment at the edge of town, as had the other groups of forest people. Molly noted her surroundings so that she would be able to find her way back to their site. It wouldn't do for a Galeing to get lost among all these forest folk and be wandering around in a strange village. She worried about how she would be received by all the new people in which she would come in contact.

After their tent was pitched and their pull cart unloaded, Granny shooed Molly away from the camp. "Go find Ronan and Elgin and have some fun. There is a lot to see in the trading market. I'm going to rest for a while and join the activities tonight," she said.

Molly walked hesitantly around the edge of town avoiding the areas where the most activity seemed to be. She was relieved when no one seemed to take any notice of her. Her plan was to catch the edge of the river and walk along it until she came to the waterfalls and get a closer look at them. She was just starting to relax and enjoy her stroll when she heard someone yell, "Look out!" She was hit squarely in the back by a force strong enough to knock her to the ground, and the next moment was lying face down in the dirt with something heavy on her back, pinning her down.

As she struggled to remove the heavy weight and sit up, she heard a feminine voice saying, "Oops...excuse me...I'm so sorry...let me get my foot loose...oh, no!" The harder the unseen attacker struggled, the worst the two seemed to become entangled. They rolled about on the ground trying to extract themselves from one another. Molly's hair became snagged on a wooden button on the stranger's clothing, and they were bound together in an awkward position.

"Bumble, what on earth are ye doing to me friend?" Ronan's voice was laced with barely-concealed laughter.

"I seem to have caused a small mishap, and now we are impossibly caught," Bumble answered.

"Hold still, ye two. Ye are just making it worse," he said. After several moments, he managed to get them loose, and the two sat on the ground blinking at one another in surprise. "Molly, meet my cousin, Bumble. She's an accident waiting to happen, but we manage to keep her from harming anyone fatally."

Bumble smiled broadly at Molly and said, "'Tis a fine day for a festival, and Ronan has spoken of ye often. I'm pleased to make yer acquaintance."

Bumble looked to be about Molly's age and had a dimpled smile that was open and friendly. She wore a pastel yellow dress made of fabric that was gauzy and flowed as she moved. Her features were elfin, but she did not have long hair like the women of Hickory Hollow. Her hair was short and tousled, and her pointed ears were easily seen peeking out from her blonde locks.

Ronan was still chuckling as he hauled each girl to her feet and brushed the dirt from her clothes. "Yer lucky Molly dinna take a swing at ye. She's quite the brawler, ye know. How did the two of ye end up in a pile anyway?"

"I crash landed," Bumble answered simply as if that were all the explanation necessary.

Molly finally spoke up, "Crash landed?"

"Aye...I do that from time to time," Bumble said.

Ronan laughed at Molly's confused expression. "Bumble is a fairy."

"The kind with wings?"

Ronan nodded.

"Where are they?" she asked, since no wings were evident. Bumble promptly turned around, and Molly saw what looked to be two small, flat-folded packages on her back. As she watched, the packages unfolded with a rustling sound and became amazingly large wings. The wings were iridescent and shone in the sunlight with a thousand colors. They fluttered gently on Bumble's back, and Molly could see that her dress had small slits to accommodate them.

Molly was unaware that her mouth hung open until Ronan spoke, "Close yer mouth, Molly May. Ye are catching flies."

Bumble folded her wings back into place and turned to face them both. She slipped one arm around Molly's shoulder in a friendly manner. "Now donna ye go to teasing her, ye rascal. She's me new friend, and I aim to show her a good time during the Gathering."

Molly recovered her composure and lifted her chin while looking at Ronan with a haughty expression. Copying the forest peoples' accent she said, "Aye...we lasses will be browsing the trade market for shiny baubles, and we shan't need any uncouth lads trailing about beggin' for our attention."

Ronan rolled his eyes comically, threw up his hands and replied with a grin, "I know when I'm not wanted. Besides...I think there's a barrel waiting to be tapped." He turned on his heel and headed toward the center of town. Bumble and Molly looked at each other and burst into laughter at the streaks of dirt that decorated their faces. They helped each other remove the traces of dust and grime and become presentable again.

"Do you fly everywhere you go?" Molly asked inquisitively.

"Fairies canna fly a long distance, and we find walking to be a convenient way to get around much of the time. Ye have really never seen fairy folk before?"

Molly shook her head. "Everyone in my world is very much like me. We come in different shapes and sizes, but no one has wings. There are so many things about the forest people that are strange and unusual to me. It is all very fascinating. What is it like to fly?"

For an answer, Bumble slipped her arm around Molly's waist and gently lifted her into the air. She headed for a tree near the center of town, deposited her on a limb and then took a seat beside her. Molly was amazed at the slender girl's strength. Although by now she should be expecting the unexpected…considering the circumstances. From their perch in the tree, they could see everything that was going on in town. Molly could see all the encampments on the edge of town, and Bumble pointed out where the fairies had set up their tents.

"Elgin told me of how ye came to be a visitor in his village. He said that Granny saved ye with an enchantment, or ye would have died from the fey fever."

"Granny has been good to me...so have Elgin and Ronan. They have come to my rescue more than once. They remind me so much of my brothers."

"What is ye world like?"

While Molly tried to describe her life and her world, the girls watched the forest people visiting and milling about and a small band of musicians tuning up in the center of town. Bumble nodded toward the gnomes who were rolling barrels out of wooden push carts. "Keep yer eye on the gnomes...they are always good for a laugh...very entertaining they are...the best makers of spiced rum, and they like to drink about as much as they make."

The gnomes that Bumble indicated were short and thick in body. They had short arms and legs, and the men folk sported long beards and bushy eyebrows. One of the barrels rolled off the cart and down a small hill, and the girls giggled as they watched the gnomes chase it some distance before it was rescued. They promptly set the barrel up on a table where a spout was tapped into it, and full mugs were passed around. Within the hour, the gnomes were singing loudly along with the musicians and arm wrestling anyone who came along and accepted the challenge. Each winner was rewarded, of course, with a full mug as his prize.

The girls spent hours sitting in the tree conversing and sharing stories about their respective worlds. Bumble described her village for Molly, and Molly did likewise with her family's summer house on the edge of the forest. They watched the activities taking place in the town square: a cloth weaving demonstration, a knife throwing contest and various games being played by young children.

The day wore on into evening, and Elgin and Ronan emerged from the crowd to coax the girls down from the tree. They escorted Bumble and Molly to supper which was a grand feast to kick off the festival. Every village contributed sumptuous dishes to the meal, and Molly sampled as many as she could. She questioned many of the ladies who had prepared them about the various ingredients and spices used and made mental notes of her favorites. The meal was followed by music, songs and storytelling. Molly could not remember when she had laughed so hard. She completely forgot to be self-conscious about being a stranger. In fact, for the first time ever, she forgot about her home and family and let herself become one of the forest people in mind and spirit.

The hour was late when the celebration finally ended and everyone drifted toward their campsites. The four friends made plans to attend some of the activities the next day, and Elgin announced that he would see Bumble to the fairy camp. Ronan looked at Molly and grinned, "Come on, Molly May. That leaves me to walk ye home. Ye tend to get lost in yer own backyard, ye know, and Granny will skin me alive if I were to let that happen." He linked his arm with hers, and they headed off in the direction of Hickory Hollow Camp.

"You're just afraid a goblin will jump out at you from the shadows…don't worry…I won't let him get you. Just hide behind me and try not to whimper," Molly teased back. As they walked along, she hummed and sang the parts that she could remember of the songs she had heard tonight.

When they reached her tent, Ronan said, "Donna forget that we're meeting Bumble and Elgin on the town square at noon tomorrow. We donna want to miss the archery contest in the afternoon. Elgin has a good chance of winning this year." Then he did the most amazing thing….the most amazing and unexpected thing. He leaned forward and gave her a lingering kiss on the cheek. When he pulled back, his green eyes looked into her shocked ones, and he softly said, "Sweet dreams, `Alainn Rua."

Young Molly with the deep auburn curls and the mismatched eyes stood still as a statue, staring at Ronan's retreating back that was disappearing into the night. When she finally let out the breath she was holding, she replied quietly to the darkness, "I'm not sure what you said, but I sure liked the way you said it."

Chapter 17

Molly spent the next morning browsing through the trade market. The forest people spread their wares on blankets for perusal, and it was much like a garage sale or flea market back home. No money changed hands, though, and anything could be, and was, traded for the items on display. It just took a little friendly haggling and bargaining back and forth, and then the deal was struck. Molly saw many unique and unusual items that interested her, and she was glad that she'd brought her baskets for bartering. She found a shawl that she thought Granny would like. It was appliquéd with colorful birds and edged with fringe. She traded a basket and some healing herbs for it with little problem. Next, she traded an extra-large basket for a pair of soft leather slippers for Bumble and a felt hat for Elgin. The slippers were dyed a soft green and scalloped around the top giving them a feminine appearance. The hat was a light gray beret that sported a bright red feather, and Molly could imagine how snappy Elgin would look wearing it.

She took her time shopping for Ronan and knew the instant she had found the perfect gift. It took her last two baskets and three healing potions to trade for the wooden flute. The back of the flute was carved with a landscape that showed Misty Falls Village. The artist had caught the picturesque scene just as Molly had first encountered it as she and her travel companions had emerged from the forest two days ago. She was pleased with her purchases and wasn't quite sure when she would give the gifts to her new-found family and friends. For the time being, she took them back to her tent and wrapped them each in a separate bundle and tied them with string. She tagged each with the recipient's name before hiding them among her personal belongings.

She arrived at noon in the village square carrying a basket of food for the picnic and spotted her trio of friends immediately. They were waiting at the base of the tree that the girls had sat in yesterday. Bumble flashed a dimpled smile as she spoke teasingly, "The boys here were worried that a good-lookin' gnome had come along and swept ye off yer feet, but I told them that ye preferred unbecoming faces such as theirs!"

Molly laughed at her joke, and the four of them started strolling toward the waterfall. They spread a blanket on the ground by the swift-moving stream and laid out their lunch. Elgin had brought roasted meat and fresh bread; Bumble had grapes and berries to share. Ronan produced a crock jug of fruit juice, and Molly pulled apple pastries from her basket and presented them with a flourish. The group had a fine time laughing, talking and dining by the stream under the shade of a leafy oak. Others had the same idea of lunching by the stream on such a beautiful day. Many families could be seen under the shade trees on the edge of the village but within viewing distance of the beautiful waterfall, and the distant squeals of children's laughter reached their ears.

After some time, Bumble spotted some other fairies further upstream and wandered off to visit with them. Elgin and Ronan decided to visit the trade market in hopes of purchasing spare arrows for the afternoon's contest. Molly turned down their invitation to go and promised that she would remain on the blanket with the picnic items. "I've already been through the market. You two go ahead. Bumble will be back shortly, and I'll be fine right here."

The peace and quiet was a welcome change from the bustle of the town, and Molly breathed a sigh of contentment. She kicked off her shoes, lay back on the blanket and felt all her muscles start to relax. It was a pleasant sensation like none other. As a warm breeze wafted over her, the far-away roar of the falls enhanced her languid state. Leaves in the tree above her rustled softly and danced in the air causing the dappled light to flicker, lulling her into a light doze. As the minutes passed, her light doze became a deep sleep, and she dreamed that the rustling of the leaves was a secret message of great importance.

Loud voices and frantic shouts awoke her from her nap. She sat up abruptly and looked wildly about. She saw people running alongside the stream and pointing. Then she spotted what had caused such alarm, and her heart seized up in terror. A small head of curly blond hair was bobbing like a cork in the middle of the fast-flowing water, and it was moving in her direction. As she watched, the head went under momentarily and then bobbed back up.

Molly grabbed the hem of her long dress and yanked it over her head, popping buttons in the process. She was now clothed in a short, thin, slip-like garment and could run toward the stream unencumbered. She watched the small head as it swept toward her and prayed that her timing was right as she bailed off into the water. It was ice cold, but she was so intent on reaching the child that she did not feel it. As the baby was swept by, she grabbed the back of his shirt and wound her hand into the cloth.

There was no way to swim in such deep, fast moving water, so she concentrated on keeping the baby's head above water and came up from time to time to get a breath for herself. It was like trying to swim in a washing machine. She felt herself bounce off a big rock and tried to stay on her back with her feet pointing downstream so that she could push off the next big rock she encountered with her legs and hopefully protect them both from injury. When she heard the baby wail loudly above the rush of the water, she rejoiced. If he could scream and cry, then his lungs weren't full of water. Now she just had to somehow make it to the shore. All those summers spent swimming at the local lake with her brothers were paying off.

Like an answered prayer, she saw a small tree directly ahead that had fallen into the stream. The base of the tree lie on the bank with its top stretched out over the water. As they moved past it, she kicked hard and closed the short gap. She held on to a branch of the treetop with one hand and kept the baby's head above water with the other. She managed to get her whole arm over the branch and hung on for dear life. She heard shouts and cries and saw a figure running nimbly along the limb, coming to their rescue. It was none other than Fenella.

As the limb became too thin to stand on, Fenella threw herself in a prone position and stretched out her arm, straining to reach the two.

"Take the baby!" Molly gasped. Fenella grabbed the child by the shirt just as Molly's small branch snapped in two. As she was swept away downstream, Fenella pulled the child from the water. She watched as Fenella sat up on the limb and clutched the baby to her chest. The last thing she saw was the fearful expression on Fenella's face looking after her, and then she was swept around a bend in the stream.

The adrenaline rush that Molly had previously experienced was now gone, and her strength was fading fast. She once again pointed her feet downstream and tried to float on her back to save energy. She hit a particularly rough patch of water that sucked her under and was tumbled over and over until she wasn't sure in which direction to swim to the surface. She did finally fight her way to the top and replenished her lungs with oxygen. The episode left her feeling weak, and she knew the temperature of the water was having an effect on her. As she passed a large boulder that was partially submerged, she clawed at it frantically trying to gain a handhold, but it was too smooth. Her heart sank as she was swept further downstream, and she knew with certainty that she was losing the battle for her life.

Chapter 18

Another rough patch of water pulled Molly under once again, and held her beneath the surface longer this time. Her left knee painfully scraped a rock, and she was rolled head over heels by the strong force of the undercurrent. She didn't have the strength to fight much longer and was growing desperate for air. She was now in a mindless state of terror, and she fought the swirling water like a madman. Her sense of direction was gone, and there seemed to be no surface.

With her lungs oxygen starved, she felt herself losing consciousness. From out of nowhere a strong pair of hands grasped her under the armpits and hauled her to the surface. She gratefully sucked in a breath of fresh air and felt herself being hoisted onto a large rock. She sprawled spread eagle and face down on the round boulder that sat midstream and sobbed in relief. It was some time before she regained her composure.

She finally lifted her head and looked around for her rescuer. At first she could not see anyone, but then she saw something splash a few feet in front of her. A head slowly rose out of the water and gave her a tentative smile. The creature's skin was such light blue in color that it was almost white. It had gills behind its ears and down its neck and wore no clothes that she could see.

She didn't know if it could understand her, but she reached out her hand palm up and softly said, "Thank you." The creature nodded in understanding and moved closer to put its palm against hers. Molly sucked in her breath and looked deep into ice blue eyes. The world fell away, and she found herself flooded with feelings of goodwill and kindness. The spell was broken when the creature moved back and dove under the water. Molly glimpsed a fish-like tail as it swam away and stared across the water for several moments hoping that it would resurface again.

"Molly!" a voice shouted. "She's over here, and she's alive!" Bumble swooped down from above followed by several other fairies. As she sat up, Bumble grasped her around the waist and flew away from the boulder across the short distance to the shore. As their feet touched the earth, Molly's legs gave out, and she slid to the ground. She was shivering even though the sun was shining brightly, and one of the fairies wrapped a shawl around her shoulders. Within minutes, she was surrounded by people who had followed the fairy search party on foot.

"Just let me rest a few minutes. I'll be fine," she told the growing crowd of onlookers. "Is the baby alright?"

"He's safe in his mum's arms, thanks to ye," answered Bumble.

Just then Elgin and Ronan arrived on the scene. Ronan's face was a thundercloud as he knelt on the ground in front of her. He grasped her by the arms and gave her a small shake. "Are ye daft, girl? What were ye thinking? Ye know to never go in the water."

Molly looked at him in confusion. "No, I don't know that. I'm not an elf. I'm a Galeing, and we go swimming all the time." The entire crowd grew silent at her remarks, and she looked up at their faces which were wearing a variety of expressions. Some looked awed; some looked shocked, and others raised their eyebrows in disbelief. She wasn't sure if they were shocked at the fact that she was a Galeing or by the fact that Galeings could swim.

Ronan laughed weakly and a rueful smile appeared on his face. "I guess I did forget for a moment that ye aren't an elf." He studied the ground before he spoke again. "The forest people sink like stones and never take chances with water like ye did."

"Fenella did. She climbed out on a small limb and grabbed the child just in time. She took a big risk," Molly said. She could see the people nodding in agreement and heard "ayes" from many. "Not all of the forest people have to steer clear of deep water. If fact, something…or someone in the water…pulled me out and left me on a big rock in the middle of the stream before swimming away," she continued.

Everyone looked at each other in puzzlement for a few minutes before the answer dawned on them. “A water sprite!” said Elgin. “It was a water sprite!”

The looks of awe were back on everyone’s faces. “What did it look like?” someone asked, and Molly did her best to describe her rescuer.

“Surely you’ve seen them for yourselves,” she said.

Bumble answered for the entire crowd. “The water sprites keep to themselves and are rarely seen. We dinna know any lived in this stream. They canna leave the water to visit dry land, and we canna enter the water, so our paths rarely cross. We’ve mostly heard stories about them from the old ones of our villages.”

Molly thought back to the moment that her eyes had stared into the ice blue ones and the unspoken messages that had passed between them…her feelings of gratitude had been met by feelings of warmth and gentleness. Her thoughts were interrupted when Elgin spoke, “Let’s get her back to camp, so she can rest for a while. The danger has passed, and she looks as though she’s had enough excitement for now.”

She realized that she was bone weary as she struggled to stand. Ronan put an arm around her for support, and they skirted the town as they headed toward her village’s campsite. Molly was relieved that they avoided the town and the curious eyes of everyone at the Gathering. She was sure her disheveled appearance would draw lots of attention, and she just wanted to crawl into bed and close her eyes.

Granny was waiting for her in the door of the tent. The story of the baby’s rescue had already spread throughout the town and surrounding encampments. Granny took control of the situation and shooed her friends away saying that Molly would be resting for some time. She helped Molly change into dry clothes and handed her a cup of warm herb tea as she sat on her cot. By the time she drained the cup, Molly’s eyelids were drooping, and she wondered what Granny had doctored the tea with to make her feel so warm, cozy and relaxed. She laid her head on her pillow and slipped into dreamless sleep.

Hours later when she awoke, she felt rested and much better. As she moved about the tent, she realized that she was slightly sore from the beating that she took from crashing into the rocks in the water.

Granny gave her a tonic that would help with the soreness, and she answered all of Granny's questions concerning the whole ordeal. Molly discovered that the baby was a gnome. His mother's name was Shonta and was Fenella's cousin. She was beginning to understand that all the forest people were related in one way or the other, and that was how they were able to move so easily from village to village and live in harmony with each other.

Granny heard voices outside the tent and went to the doorway to investigate. "Molly, I think someone has come to pay ye a visit."

Molly stepped outside the tent and realized a small group of gnomes were gathered around. Shonta was holding the rescued babe and stepped forward when Molly appeared. Without a word she placed the toddler in Molly's arms. The tiny child began to squeal in delight, jabbering and patting Molly's face, and she cooed back to the baby in a nonsensical language.

Funny how we turn into blithering idiots when we are around little ones, and this sweet darling could melt the coldest of hearts.

Shonta put her hand on Molly's neck and pulled her head down to hers. She pressed her forehead to Molly's in commiseration for several seconds and then turned and walked back to the group of gnomes who patted Shonta's back in a comforting manner.

Molly was totally entranced with the petite baby she was holding and did not notice that something was afoot for several minutes. Shonta looked miserable and Fenella, right behind her, was wearing a sorrowful expression.

That's the first time I've seen something other than hostility on that face.

Molly took the baby's little arm and waved it at Shonta, "Say 'hi' to Momma." The misery on Shonta's face only deepened. Fenella came forward and handed a bundle of clothing to Granny. Now, alarm bells were going off in her head.

"What's going on, Granny?" Molly asked.

"She is repaying yer bravery with a gift."

"I don't understand."

"Ye saved her baby, so she is giving the boy to ye."

"WHAT?"

"It is our custom. When ye save the life of a child, it becomes yers."

"Shonta is giving me her child?" Molly choked out.

"She must…it is what is expected of her."

Molly was quiet and thoughtful for several seconds as she played with the baby. "Granny, I can't keep some other woman's baby. That would be cruel. Do I have to keep him? Am I permitted to give him back?"

Granny's eyes twinkled as she replied, "Aye, it is permitted. The choice is yers."

Molly kissed the baby on the cheek, hugged it fiercely and took a few steps in Shonta's direction. She placed the wee one in Shonta's arms and smiled. "He is the most beautiful child in the world, and I thank you for the gift, but he belongs with his mother. Can I come see him from time to time?"

As the tears coursed down the little momma's face, she nodded gratefully. "Please come visit us in Mill Creek Village soon. There will always be a place for ye in our cottage."

With this, all the gnomes clustered around Shonta and nodded in agreement. The friendly little people had Molly stoop so that they could kiss both her cheeks and pat her back. They finally headed away to the center of town, and Molly stood watching them go still feeling warm and content from all the love and affection that had been showered upon her. She eventually noticed the slim, raven-haired maiden who stood alone under a tree some yards away clutching the bundle of baby clothes. When their eyes met, she nodded to Molly, silently mouthed "thank ye" and then she, too, turned and walked back toward town.

Chapter 19

The last day of the Gathering dawned bright and clear. The four friends had decided to spend the day enjoying what remained of the festivities, so they met in town right after breakfast. Elgin had won the archery contest the day before, and the other three weren't sure they would be able to tolerate him for the entire day. He strode proudly about town with his bow and quiver over his shoulder accepting congratulations from the other men. As the morning wore on, his walk became more of a swagger, and his chest was as puffed as a rooster. They arrived where the storytelling contest was being held just as it began. Bantry was the only contestant familiar to Molly, but her friends knew most of the others.

With each participant, the stories became more outrageous and hilarious. The contest was down to the final round with three storytellers left. Bantry was one of the final three, and after each of his stories, Molly and her friends clapped, hooted and hollered....cheering for the little, bearded man and showing the judges their choice for the winner. In the end, a fairy named Kean took the prize, and Bantry came in a close second.

Elgin and Ronan helped the gnome folks load some empty barrels into carts and were rewarded mincemeat pies for their trouble. They found a shady tree on the edge of the market and sat down beneath it to share their pies with Molly and Bumble. As they enjoyed their snack, a young boy came speeding by at a run. Recognizing him, Bumble called out, "Where are ye off to in such a hurry, Sean?"

"There's a mushball game starting in the meadow outside of town. Come on!" he answered over his shoulder as he continued on.

As Molly was leisurely savoring her last bite of pie, the other three quickly brushed the crumbs from their hands and jumped to their feet. Bumble grabbed her hand and yanked her upright, hustling her away from the shade tree. "Hey, what's the rush?" she grumbled as she was dragged toward the edge of town.

When they reached the meadow, teams were already being formed, and Molly found herself being designated a hitter on Heath's team. Since she didn't know what a hitter did or who Heath was, it was all very confusing. She tried to protest her involvement in the game, but her comments fell on deaf ears. The game began, and she sat on a fallen log with the other hitters.

I guess they'll discover their blunder soon enough. With my lack of athletic ability, I am usually a secret weapon for the other team.

As she watched the game, she found it rather bewildering. It seemed to be a mixture of baseball, kickball, rugby and wrestling. A leather ball, the size of a large grapefruit, was pitched or kicked to the hitter. The hitter had a flat bat, similar to the type used in cricket, and tried to knock the ball far out into the meadow. The runners had to stand with one hand on the bases, which were mushrooms, while the pitchers stood on top. Standing on top proved to be very challenging, since the mushrooms grew very fast and would move on their own without warning. They would give a shudder and sprout up several inches, sometimes tumbling the pitchers to the ground.

The outfielders stayed outside the mushroom circle and retrieved the ball should it make it that far. Points were earned when a runner made it around the entire circle. The ball could be wrestled from an opposing team member or intercepted in mid-air. The runners were elves since they were light on their feet. The pitchers were gnomes since they had strong throwing arms, and the outfielders were fairies who could use their flying abilities to catch airborne balls. Hitters could be anyone. When it was Molly's turn up to bat, she gritted her teeth and said under her breath, "Here goes nothing."

Her one swing connected with air and she returned to her seat on the log to watch the game. When her turn once more, she struck out yet again. On her third time up to bat, she decided to change tactics as she had seen the other hitters do. At the last minute, she lowered the bat and kicked at the ball with all her might. Her foot connected with….nothing.

In her desperate effort to kick the ball hard, her left foot joined the right up in the air, and she landed on her back in the dust. To her humiliation, her dress had flown upward also and covered her head. She slowly sat up and started pulling her dress down. *Thank goodness for underwear….now I think I shall crawl off into the woods and die.*

She could hear the laughter before the dress cleared her head, and sat for several seconds looking at the players on the field. They covered their mouths to hide the unbidden giggles. Some looked away…obviously finding something interesting in the forest to study while they fought to maintain control. Bumble flew to her side and helped her to her feet. While she tried to show concern, the sides of her mouth kept creeping up, and a snicker or two escaped. Molly had to acknowledge the hilarity of the situation, and as soon as she was steady on her feet once again, she chuckled also. This caused the floodgates to open, and seeing her laugh at herself, gave everyone else permission to lose control. One gnome laughed so hard that he fell off his mushroom. It was several minutes before the players could stop cackling and wipe their eyes. Red-faced, Molly stood very still and then performed a dramatic bow, lifted her chin and marched comically back to the log to sit. This caused the entire meadow to erupt into fresh laughter so that the game was delayed once again.

At this point, Molly was determined to just sit out the rest of the game, but no one would hear of it. They coaxed her into switching to the position of runner, and she managed to run four of the mushroom bases before she was tagged out. She gladly joined the ranks of the other runners who had been tagged and watched the rest of the game from the sidelines. Unfortunately, the other team won…although Molly couldn't figure out just how, since she stayed thoroughly baffled by the whole sporting event.

Everyone headed back to town hungry and thirsty and excited

from the game. Molly's antics had alleviated the embarrassment she had previously experienced, and many players slapped her on the back for being such a good sport. The four friends found cool drinks back in town and grabbed an empty makeshift table at which to sit in the trading market. Ronan grinned at her over his full mug and just shook his head. "Molly May, I have to truly say that there is no one like ye in the world."

Bumble slid over and threw her arm around Molly. "Of course she is one of a kind. That is why we are forever friends."

"Just tell me that we won't be playing anymore sports for a while. An athlete I am not. Back home I am always the last one chosen on a team, and sometimes a fight breaks out between the team captains about who will be forced to take me," she wryly confessed.

"I can see why," said Elgin with a smile.

"How about coming to my village for a few days, Molly? I'm sure ye could use a break from these two insolent lads here," said Bumble.

"That would be great…of course, I'd have to check with Granny first," Molly replied.

Bumble spent the next few minutes describing her village, and Molly grew excited at the thought of a town full of tree houses. From what she could understand, the fairy people built their dwellings in the trees instead of on the ground. She grew very excited at the prospect of seeing Willow Grove Village. After agreeing to meet Elgin and Ronan for that afternoon's dance, Bumble and Molly hurried off to find Granny and to get ready for the finale soirée of the gathering.

As the two young men sat watching after the departing figures, Elgin looked at Ronan and said, "So…when are ye going to tell Molly how ye feel about her?"

"Is it that apparent to everyone?" he asked in return.

"Just to us who know ye best."

Ronan sighed. "I guess I knew she was the one for me when I woke in Granny's cottage and found her sleeping in the chair beside my bed. She looked at me with those amazing eyes, and I knew my life would never be the same."

After several minutes of silence, Elgin grinned and slapped Ronan on the back. "Well, she sure isn't a mushball player of any sort," he said teasingly.

"Who cares?" Ronan said wearing a lopsided grin…his eyes still trained on Molly in the distance.

"What fills the eye fills the heart…aye?" asked Elgin.

"Aye," Ronan agreed with a nod.

Chapter 20

Granny was agreeable to the idea of Molly spending a few days with Bumble in Willow Grove Village. Since no one had reported any attacks by the goblins lately, it looked as though the threat was over for now. The girls planned for Molly to leave the Gathering with Bumble and, after a few days, return to Hickory Hollow with Elgin, Ronan and a few other young men as escorts. The girls were excited over Molly's visit and parted reluctantly as Bumble headed to her own tent to dress for the afternoon's dance.

"Have ye enjoyed the Gathering, Molly dear?" asked Granny.

"It has been an adventure…that's for sure," answered Molly. "So many new things to see and do…new people to meet….the water sprites are especially interesting. There is nothing like them in my world."

After a moment of silence, Molly asked, "Granny, have you ever been to my world?"

"Goodness no, child…although I have caught glimpses of it down through the years. Our respective worlds exist side by side, but it is rare for them to cross….I guess ye are the exception…aye, that makes ye special…ye seem to be able to see our world from yer own, and we were able to bring ye into ours to rescue ye."

Molly gazed out the doorway of the tent, and her gaze seemed to be locked onto something far away. "The longer I stay here…the harder it will be to return to my world. I feel my home and family slipping further away from my grasp. I'm having a difficult time even remembering my brothers' faces."

Granny stood behind Molly, who was sitting in a chair. She picked up a hair brush and tenderly drew it through her curly locks.

"Then perhaps, child, someone else's face is occupying yer thoughts these days."

It occurred to Molly that this motherly gesture came so natural to Granny and that she could not remember a time when her own mother had done this simple thing for her. As Granny stroked and brushed her hair, she was filled with love for the elderly woman who had adopted her as her own child. *So this is what it feels like to have a mother's love.* She was filled with joy but also with anguish for having been denied this love for so long by her own mother. A thought rose unbidden to mind…if she had to choose between this world and the other, which would she pick? As soon as the thought came, she banished it in a panic. *Best not to think on such things*. Granny had said that when the time was right the magic would send her back.

"I have a surprise for ye," said Granny, placing a package in Molly's lap.

Molly looked at the package and then looked at Granny in puzzlement.

"Aren't ye going to open it?" Granny asked.

Molly untied the string and unfolded the wrapping. Inside was a beautiful, teal dress made of some type of fabric that was unlike anything she had ever seen. There was handmade lace around the neck and sleeves and tiny rosebuds embroidered on the bodice. Molly could only stare in wonder.

"Put it on…I knew ye would need something to wear to the dance tonight, and I had Meadow start working on it weeks ago."

"Granny, it's beautiful. What is this fabric?"

"It is made of woven spider silk….a skill Meadow learned from the fairies. We both thought the color would be striking with yer hair and eyes."

Molly's chin started to tremble. Tears threatened to spill from her eyes at the thought of what such a fine gift must have cost Granny and how she had planned weeks ahead to make sure Molly would enjoy the dance in such a stunning creation.

"Now, now, child…donna get yer new dress wet…put it on, put it on."

Molly went behind the curtain hung for privacy and slipped it over her head. It fit her perfectly. The dress flared at the hips and seemed to float when she walked from behind the curtain. Granny's eyes lit up, and she nodded approvingly. "Sit and let me wind this matching ribbon in yer hair."

A few short minutes later, Molly's unruly hair was tamed into an upswept style entwined with ribbon and a few sprigs of tiny flowers. Small, loose curls framed her face and completed the effect. Just then, Bumble swept into the tent unannounced and stopped in startled surprise. "Look at ye!" she breathed in awe.

"The dress was a gift from Granny…isn't it just gorgeous?" Molly's eyes filled again, and she put her arms around the old woman. "No one has ever given me such a wonderful gift. I have something for you, too." She reached under her cot and pulled out the package that was labeled with Granny's name.

It was her turn to surprise Granny who looked at the package in wonder. "Well…open it," she said.

When Granny saw the shawl decorated with the bird design, she beamed with pleasure. She slipped it over her shoulders and said, "Looks like we'll both be sporting new lovelies tonight. The last night of the Gathering is always the best, so it should be quite an evening. Now ye girls run along and find the boys. I'll be there shortly."

The girls put the finishing touches on their appearances and headed down the path to town. They linked arms and talked excitedly in anticipation of the evening. Bumble caught her foot on a root and nearly landed in the dirt, but she was saved by their linked arms. Molly caught her just in time, and they laughed hysterically at their combined clumsiness. "How many guys are we going to cripple tonight while dancing?" Molly quipped. "I think after we step on the first pair of toes, we will find ourselves sitting on the sidelines watching all the fun for the rest of the evening."

"Then we will just dance with each other!" said Bumble with resolve.

"I think we did that the day we met…." replied Molly, and they both broke into giggles again remembering the collision that left them entangled and rolling on the ground.

"Look out, lads, here we come!" declared Bumble as they stepped into the glade where the dance was being held.

The girls stopped short as they gazed around in awe attempting to take in the entire scene. Arching branches from hardwood trees formed a ceiling over the glade. Flowering vines had grown along the limbs, and yellow blossoms hung from overhead, creating natural decorations for the festive occasion. It seemed all the forest people were attending the final event of the gathering. There was a group of musicians playing a rollicking song while a large crowd of people danced. Around the edge of the glade were logs and benches for sitting and tables groaning under the weight of food. While the dancers twirled and dipped in their colorful finery, dusk began to settle over the glade. Several fairies began flitting overhead among the arching branches, distributing hanging lanterns that added to the enchanted atmosphere of the party. A young man spotted the two attractive girls standing on the edge of the activity and pointed them out to his friends. After some encouragement from the group, two of the braver lads broke away from the cluster and approached the girls.

"Will ye be dancing this evening, ladies?"

The girls had barely nodded when they were grabbed by the hands and swept into the melee of the dancing. Their partners were quite adept at all the intricate steps and led them through the rousing number. As the song ended, they found themselves presented with new partners eager to take a turn on the dance floor. One dance ran into another and the changing of partners became a blur. Molly chatted with a sweet-faced gnome who only came to her shoulders in height but was a gentlemanly and gracious partner. He was one of Shonta's relatives and had been anxious to meet her. When the dance ended, she proclaimed her thirst and begged a reprieve from the next young man who was waiting to twirl her about the dance floor. He bowed gallantly, then asked to dance with her later and she consented. She made her way to the table that held refreshments and tried to catch her breath. As she sipped fruit juice, she spotted Bumble among the dancers and smiled and waved. She was having a marvelous time. Surely this was more fun than a high school prom. She leaned against a tree and watched the celebration going on all around her. Her heart was glad, and her eyes were sparkling in the flickering light of the lanterns overhead.

"Those are truly the most remarkable eyes I have ever seen," said a voice in her ear as a hand reached around in front of her holding a pink wildflower.

"Thanks…they came with the face," she quipped as she took the flower. She turned and looked up at Ronan's smiling face. "Where have you been?"

"Right here all evening…hoping to get a dance with ye."

"Well….you're a bit tardy…all of my dances have already been promised," she teased.

"I'll just be a rude fella then and break in line." Saying this, he plucked the flower from her, tucked it behind her ear and took her by the hand, leading her into the crowd just as a new dance started.

Chapter 21

The evening continued with hours of feasting and dancing. After dancing with Ronan a time or two, Molly was claimed by other young men, and Ronan had to move fast to outmaneuver the lads vying for her attention. Eventually, the others drifted away looking to dance with other girls when it was evident that Ronan was planning to monopolize Molly for the rest of the evening. Bumble and Elgin found them in the crowd, and Elgin grinned like the cat that ate the canary.

"Well…I see ye finally beat the other fellas off. Did she perhaps remember yer name, or did ye have to reintroduce yerself?"

"What do you mean by that? Rodney and I have been having a wonderful time…I mean…Roger and I…no, that's not right…Ricky?...Randall?" Molly looked up quizzically at Ronan in pretend confusion while Bumble snickered.

"It seems I have not made much of an impression if the fair maiden cannot remember my name. I shall remedy that at once…M'lady," Ronan said with a bow, and grabbing her hand he headed for the center of the dancing crowd just as the pace of the music changed. A man with a beautiful tenor voice began singing a love song, and the dancing slowed to match the rhythm. Molly and Ronan danced looking at each other until Ronan's gaze caused her to look away in embarrassment.

"What are ye thinking, Molly May?"

Molly took several seconds to answer. "Sometimes this place seems like a dream…like I'm not really here…like it is all a wonderful fantasy…"

When Ronan spoke again, he did so very slowly and thoughtfully. "And do I seem real? Cause I assure ye that I am…I know that this world is so different from yer own, but if ye canna go back…would it be so terrible to stay here?"

Before Molly could answer, the song ended, and the musicians took a break. Molly and Ronan joined everyone else at the tables covered in food, and the famished crowd feasted on the various dishes that had been prepared. The forest people mixed and mingled, conversing and laughing until the dancing started again.

This time, the musicians started with a dance called Damsel's Desire, and Bumble quickly explained how the dance worked. All the ladies were expected to join hands and form a large circle. As the circle moved around the edge of the dance area, the men formed an even larger circle around the outside of the ladies and moved in the opposite direction. When a girl spotted someone with whom she wished to dance, she reached out, snatched him from his circle and finished the dance in the middle of the dance area.

Molly and Bumble took their places in the formation, and the dance started. Bumble grabbed Elgin in the first pass, and Ronan grinned expectantly at Molly across the way. Molly let Ronan pass twice before she made her move. As he came around again, she reached out and deliberately grabbed the elderly gnome who was right beside Ronan. The little fellow was wrinkled with a long, white beard, mustache and small tufts of hair above his ears. Most of the dancers caught on to Molly's joke, including her dance partner, and he grinned appreciatively up at Molly as he danced her about the glade. When the dance was over, Molly took him by the hand and walked him courteously to his waiting wife, who was smiling broadly at the jest. Since she had most everyone's attention, Molly plucked the little man's hat from his head, kissed his bald pate and returned his hat to its rightful place. The crowd that had been chuckling before now roared with laughter.

As the music started again, Ronan took Molly's arm and led her to one of the benches to sit for a spell. His eyes were twinkling with amusement as he spoke, "Ye are full are surprises, Molly May. I never know what ye are up to. I, too, have a surprise for ye." He reached into his pocket and pulled out a metal bracelet that was cast to look like intertwining vines and flowers. He put it on her wrist saying, "It reminds me of the day we took a swing on the vines in the forest."

"That seems so long ago, and yet it seems like yesterday. Time really does work differently here." Watching the dancers, but with her mind on something else, she asked, "Ronan…if I were to stay here, would I stay young for hundreds of years like the forest people…I mean…like you?"

Ronan searched her face before answering, "I would think that in our world ye would live within this time… just as we do….but Granny might know the answer to that. She and a few others have lived a very long time and know the magic of the forest."

Molly looked at the bracelet on her arm and smiled at Ronan. "It is a wonderful gift, and I will always think of you when I look at it."

Bumble and Elgin came dancing by about that moment. "Come on! Time's a wastin', and there's dancin' to be done!"

Molly and Ronan dashed back into the throng and danced until the last song was played. As the last chords faded, one of the men from Misty Falls Village stood in front of the musicians and clapped his hands for everyone's attention. "It's been a fine Gathering this year, and we thank ye all for coming. 'Tis a fine thing to be reacquainted with kith and kin and do some sharing and fellowshipping with one another. We have partaken of good food and had many a laugh with ye all. May ye be blessed and safe from harm. May the memories of these days be pleasin'. May the magic of the forest watch over ye as ye journey home on the morrow."

The crowd answered with cries of "Here, here!…Farewell everyone!...Until we meet again!"

As the forest people heartily embraced those around them and exchanged pecks on the cheeks, a young woman's clear voice came weaving through the noise of the crowd. The throng fell silent to hear her song as she stood in front of the forest people. Ronan slipped his arms around Molly's waist, and she leaned back into his embrace and swayed to the music as many in the crowd did. The young woman's sweet sound caused conflicting feelings of joy and nostalgia for everyone within hearing.

"Home is in the deep woods surrounded by the trees
That whisper secrets to the wind in the rustling of the leaves.

So it has been for many a year, and many a year shall be,
And it is my heart's desire that home once more I see.
I've wandered far across the hills....across the countless miles.
I've sailed the seas and walked upon strange and foreign isles.
But that world is not my own. I long for those elsewhere.
Should I reach deep woods again, I'll be forever there.
Aye, I shall be forever there."

As the last note echoed in the woods, the musicians packed away their instruments, and fairies flitted overhead extinguishing the candles in the lanterns. The forest people said their final goodbyes, turned and headed back to their camps. The Gathering was officially over, and in the morning, all the visitors would pack up and make the journey back to their villages.

Bumble, Elgin and Ronan walked Molly back to her tent and bid her goodnight. She slipped into bed quietly since Granny was already asleep and snoring softly on her cot. Her head was full of excitement from the dance and for tomorrow when she would visit Bumble's village. As she fingered the beautiful bracelet on her wrist, a certain young man with a tan face, dark eyes and dark, curly hair was impossible to get out of her mind. Sometime later when she finally drifted off, Crionna called softly from the tree outside the tent, "Who…Who?" to which Molly answered by whispering, "Ronan," in her sleep.

Chapter 22

Even though the forest people had danced late into the night, they arose at dawn and quickly disassembled their camps. Goodbyes had already been said, so groups of visitors quickly disappeared into the forest with their backpacks and pull carts. No one was traveling alone, because the possibility of a goblin attack was still a concern. Although the goblin sightings had been scarce of late, that did not mean that they were done with their devilment. Precautions were still being taken.

Molly and Granny had their tent and belongings packed in short time, and when their escorts came to fetch them, Molly hugged Granny fiercely and promised to see her in a few days. She stood holding her small bag of clothing and watched Granny leave the clearing that held the town of Misty Falls Village. Granny paused at the edge of the forest and waved at her, and then she was gone. Molly stared after her with a lump in her throat. She already missed Granny.

What's wrong with me? I will be back in Hickory Hollow in a few days.

"Ready to go?" a voice asked. Molly turned to find Bumble standing close by. "I am so excited that ye are coming home with me."

The girls headed toward the area where the fairy camp had been, and Molly noted how much smaller the town looked without all the encampments encircling it. The girls shouldered backpacks and woven baskets with straps to help carry the belongings of the fairy people through the forest. Because the fairy people often flew, they did not use pull carts as Granny's people did. They were also unusually strong and could carry large loads of camping equipment in their arms and on their backs. Molly's backpack was not as heavy, as they were aware that she did not possess their strength. Even the children carried small bundles, and they flitted about the group, anxious to be off.

Molly and Bumble were with one of the first fairy groups to leave, and they headed into the forest at an easy pace. Molly and Bumble chatted as they walked along.

"Did ye enjoy the dance last night?" Bumble asked.

"It was wonderful," she answered. "I don't think our dances back home are nearly as much fun."

"I noticed that Ronan was quite possessive of ye…none of the other lads had a chance once he claimed yer hand."

Molly blushed and looked away before answering. "I've never had a boyfriend before…it's kind of nice."

"Never had a sweetheart?......Someone as pretty as ye?... Go on with ye now," Bumble scoffed.

"Pretty? Not in my world…I'm just ordinary Molly…no one pays any attention to me…none of the boys at my school even know I exist."

"The boys in ye world must be blind," Bumble said under her breath, shaking her head.

"Look at the bracelet that Ronan gave me last night," Molly said shyly, holding up her arm to display the metal band.

"Molly Girl! Ye are just now showing me this? What am I to do with ye?" Bumble was exasperated.

Molly just smiled and said, "A girl has to have some secrets, you know."

The morning wore on, and the girls talked for hours as they ambled along the well-worn path that led through the woods to Willow Grove Village. It was well past noon when the group stopped beneath a large shade tree to have lunch and rest for a spell. The young fairy children had too much energy to sit still after they ate lunch and chased each other about…running and swooping a few feet off the ground. When it was time to resume their journey, the group shouldered their backpacks and began walking once more.

It was early afternoon when they reached Bumble's village. Molly paused at the edge of the town and took in the surroundings in delighted surprise. "Bumble, you didn't tell me that your village was so…..," she paused as she struggled to find the right words, "….delightful!"

Indeed it was delightful…also captivating and enchanting. The fairies had built their homes in the same organic fashion as the elves except the houses were built in the trees instead of under them. Staircases and ladders led up and around the tree trunks to give access to the homes. Swinging walkways could be seen here and there connecting the houses to one another. Once more Molly found that she was experiencing that feeling of surrealism….like she was dreaming wide awake in a make-believe world.

"Come on. I'll show ye my house. We'll set up a cot in my room." Having said that, Bumble wrapped her arms around Molly's waist and lifted her off the ground, flitting through the massive branches of the trees past many of the tree houses that made up the village. She gently touched down on the deck-like porch of one of the houses. The door swung open to reveal a pretty fairy whose facial features resembled Bumble's.

"Molly, this is my sister, Clover, and this is our home…yer home, too, as long as ye wish to stay."

"It's nice to meet you, Clover. I'll try not to be any trouble while I'm here."

"Donna ye worry yer head none about that, Molly. Bumble has talked of little else since meeting ye at the Gathering. I traveled back with another group of villagers and just got back meself."

Bumble, Molly and Clover made short work of unpacking their belongings and settling Molly into Bumble's room. Like the elves, the fairies lived simply. Their homes contained the basic necessities and any adornment was handmade from items found in the forest. Clover bustled about the small kitchen area putting on a pot of soup in the fireplace, to cook for supper. Molly and Bumble went out onto the deck for a breath of fresh air. Cooking fires were being lit in the tree houses, and the stone chimneys puffed gray smoke into the evening breeze.

"Why do most of the houses have stairs and ladders since fairies can just use their wings to get from the ground up to their homes?" Molly asked quizzically.

"So our visiting kin can come and go as they please, Silly."

Molly giggled. "I suppose that would discourage guests....but it would also solve the problem of door-to-door salesmen and Girl Scouts selling cookies."

"Door-to-door what?" Bumble asked.

"Nothing important." *How do I explain those parts of my world to a fairy in this world?*

The girls visited until Clover called them in to supper. Then they wasted no time finding their beds and settling in for the night. Tired from their journey through the woods, they promptly fell asleep.

The next morning Bumble announced that she had to help some of the other fairies collect spider silk from the forest. This left Molly with no plans of her own. After breakfast, Bumble flitted away on her errand, and Clover got busy with housekeeping chores.

"Why donna ye have a look around the village?" Clover asked.

"I think I will," said Molly. "I will be back in a little while." She threw her cloak about her shoulders and descended the stairs to the ground. She wandered through the village and greeted those she saw. All the fairies nodded and smiled as they went about their work, and Molly found her stroll to be relaxing. She happened upon a group of children playing around a base of a large tree and sat down on a log to watch for a while. It was a game like Red Rover that she had played so often herself in the schoolyard. Eventually, a woman's voice called the children home, and they waved goodbye to Molly and flitted away.

Molly had failed to notice the dark clouds that had gathered in the sky, and she was startled when thunder pealed overhead. She began to hurry through the village, berating herself for staying gone so long. When the sky opened up, Molly spotted a house perched on a limb a short distance from the ground. She darted under the house just in time and avoided a soaking. She stood under the house and pulled her cloak tightly about her, because the air had grown cool with the coming of the rain. As she gazed out at the cascade of water and wondered how long it would continue, the hairs on the back of her neck stood up, and she suddenly became aware of a silent presence behind her. With a feeling of apprehension and uneasiness, she turned slowly to face whatever awaited her.

Chapter 23

Molly was face-to-face with an old man who was standing in an open doorway situated in the tree trunk that she had failed to notice. The room behind him was warm and inviting, and the yellow light poured out from behind him like liquid.

"Well…donna just stand there…come on in and warm yerself by the fire," the old man said. He stepped back into the room, holding the door open and gestured for Molly to enter.

She stepped hesitantly into the room and sat down in the chair that the stranger indicated. She felt his hands on her shoulders close to her neck, and she froze in place.

"Let me take yer cloak and hang it by the door," he said gently.

Molly relinquished her cloak and pulled the chair closer to the fire, holding out her hands to its spreading warmth. She forced herself to relax and laughed at herself for being so jumpy. She took in his long white beard and the kind eyes that peered at her.

He handed her a mug of hot spiced cider, and she sipped it gratefully. Pulling up another chair, he rested his hands on his knees and leaned forward.

"So….ye are the Molly that I have been hearing so much about."

This took her aback, and she stared into her mug several seconds before answering. "I didn't realize my visit to Willow Grove was a newsworthy event."

He smiled broadly as he talked. "Not much happens around here without everyone knowing about it, and yer visit is known to all…as well as most of the events surrounding ye at the Gathering. I guess you donna realize the celebrity ye have become."

Molly blushed to the tips of her ears. She was never comfortable being the center of attention. "I shouldn't stay too long. It might worry my friends," she stammered.

"Aaah, well...I 'spect the rain will last for a time, and I would ask that ye linger a while. I was hoping to get to speak with ye."

She took a sip of cider before asking, "What about?"

"I was just wondering if ye had begun to feel the pull of the forest magic since ye have been here."

With a sad, little smile, she answered wistfully, "I am finding it hard to recall the details of home. It's like a picture that is slowly fading. Even the faces of my family are becoming a blurred memory."

"Aye, so it is the same for ye as it was for me."

That took a moment to sink in. She looked at him quizzically for several moments, and then understanding slowly dawned. "You came from the Galeing world, too?" she asked in disbelief.

He chuckled in amusement. "Aye, I did. My name is Aiden, and I have been with the forest people so long now that most have forgotten that I was not born here. I knew sooner or later that our paths would cross, and we would have a lot to talk about."

"But you don't look like a Galeing."

"If ye stay here long enough, the forest magic changes ye."

"How did you get here? Did you become lost in the forest as I did?" Molly asked.

"Not exactly…my story is somewhat different from yers."

As the rain continued to pour outside the windows that were set into the massive, hollow tree trunk, Aiden proceeded to explain how he had come to live among the forest people. "Many, many years ago, I lived in the other world just as ye did. I owned a successful business with my best friend and had a wife and a baby boy. My business fell upon hard times and went under, and the stress caused a split with my best friend. We lost everything. I could no longer provide for my wife and child. I had to travel to find work, and in my absence, my wife and son were killed in an accident."

Aiden paused for a moment in the telling and stared into the fire, and then he cleared his throat and began again. "I had nothing left to live for. Crazy with grief and out of my mind, I stumbled into the woods and walked for days. I guess I thought I could somehow outrun the sorrow. I just wanted to disappear off the face of the earth. I finally collapsed from hunger and lost consciousness. I guess I hoped that I would just close my eyes and die so that I could join my wife and son. When I did wake days later, I was here with the forest people. They nursed me back to health, and I have been here ever since."

"Did you ever try to get back home?" Molly asked.

"Home?...Home was my wife and son….there was nothing to go back to. With help from the forest people, I regained my will to live and found a place among them. This is where I belong now. For years I have studied their magic and have learned many of the secrets of the forest."

It was Molly's turn to stare into the fire. "Sometimes I wonder if I will ever get back home…and then sometimes I wonder if I still want to. This place is enchanted…..it pulls you in and weaves a spell that is hard to resist."

"That may be a decision that ye will have to make when the time comes. Put yer mind to some serious thought, Molly. When the magic is right, ye may only have one chance before that window of opportunity closes forever. Ever since ye were brought here, the elders of all the villages have been working on how to send ye back. We have made some progress, but magic of this sort works on its own time schedule."

"Is there anything from our world that you miss?" Molly said.

"Absolutely nothing…I prefer the simple life that is practiced here. The forest people are delightful…hardworking and honest. They embody the best of mankind. They live in harmony with nature and care for one another like those from the Galeing world should."

"All except the goblins..." Molly said with a shudder.

"Aye...I did hear about yer run-in with the goblins…a nasty bunch of scoundrels, to be sure. They donna usually cause too much trouble, but they have become much braver and aggressive as of late. Something tells me that we will have to deal with them soon. They are becoming a real threat."

"Aiden…..are there any other Galeings here with the forest people?"

He looked thoughtful for several seconds before he spoke. "I think we are the only two, but I think there have been others in the far past. I believe these two worlds have always existed adjacently, but over the years the distance between them has grown. It is almost impossible for a Galeing to cross over into this world now….for ye to be here, is extraordinary, indeed."

Aiden and Molly continued sitting in front of the warm fire, sipping cider and talking until the rain stopped. When Molly noticed that the weather had cleared, she donned her cloak and headed for the door. "Guess I had better get back to Bumble and Clover, or they will send out a search party."

When she reached the door, Aiden stopped her with a hand on her shoulder, and she turned and looked into his kind eyes. In a soft voice, he bid her goodbye and said, "Nothing happens by accident, Molly. It was meant for ye to be here. No one knows for sure if ye will make it back to the other world, but whatever happens…ye will have to learn to be content with yer life and make the best of it."

Molly searched his face, but it betrayed no hidden meanings, so she nodded her agreement and ducked out the door. In the gathering dusk, she headed for Bumble's part of the village and at the last minute, stopped and looked back. Aiden was still standing in the open doorway framed in the light watching her departure. She lifted her hand in a farewell gesture, and he responded in kind, and with that, she hurried on through the coming darkness.

Chapter 24

The days passed swiftly for Molly in Willow Grove Village. The fairies were as happy and welcoming as the elves, and Molly found that their day-to-day activities were almost identical to those in Hickory Hollow. The fairies foraged in the forest for food and other necessities, tended to their children and worked at the crafts that benefited the entire village. They were known for their unusual skill of weaving spider thread into fine silk cloth, and Molly had a chance to watch a demonstration of this firsthand. She supposed this was unique to the fairies, mainly because their flying ability gave them access to spider webs high up in the trees, and it took an ample amount of spider thread to weave enough cloth to make a garment of any size.

It was still disconcerting for Molly to be standing on solid ground one moment and then swooping among the branches of an enormous tree the next. Bumble had a habit of snatching Molly up without warning and lifting her into the air when she took it into her head to dash off toward something that she wished her to see. Molly came close to upchucking her dinner more than once or twice before Bumble realized the effect it had on her.

Each day brought something new for Molly to see or do, and the girls fell into bed each night tired but too excited to sleep. They talked and giggled for hours, sometimes speculating about what Ronan and Elgin might be doing back in their respective villages. They relived the best parts of the dance on the final night of the Gathering, and Molly would lie in the dark and finger the bracelet on her wrist as they talked. When she finally fell asleep, she dreamed of an attractive face with dark eyes framed by dark, curly hair. Sometimes, he was sitting on a rock playing a flute, and other times he was whirling her about while music played. At all times, he smiled lovingly down at her, and she awoke each morning cheerful and lighthearted.

Molly sat in on "flying school" one morning that was being held in the center of the village. The young fairies that were toddling about were learning to use their wings, and there were lots of spills and tumbles as the day progressed. Molly held her breath several times as mid-air collisions almost occurred, and she found herself running around under the particularly wobbly flyers with her arms outstretched, ready to catch them should they go into a crash landing. While the experience was exhilarating, she found herself emotionally wrung out and nervous by the end of morning, and she wondered how the young mothers could endure it all so calmly. Her apparent concern for the safety of the baby fairies endeared her to the village women, and she made many new friends easily as she explored the small community.

Later that evening at nightfall, she paused on a swinging crosswalk that connected several of the tree houses. From her viewpoint she could see lights coming on in the windows of the tree houses and could hear children being called in to supper. Cooking fires sent small wisps of gray smoke from the chimneys into the vibrant sunset sky, and an air of serenity permeated the entire scene. Molly was aware of a sense of peacefulness seeping into her soul, and she sighed in contentment as she leaned on the rope railing and gazed out at the scene. An owl hooted close by, and she searched the oncoming darkness…finally making out the familiar shape on a limb. "This is the most fantastic place on Earth…isn't it, Crionna?" she said, addressing her remarks to her old friend. In reply, Crionna left her perch and flew a circle around Molly, landing on a limb much closer.

"So what is the latest news in the forest? Anything I should know about?"

Crionna blinked her eyes, ruffled her feathers and made soft chirping noises. "How can I leave this place when the time comes, but how can I not go back to my family and relieve them of their worry and grief?"

Molly continued to survey the dream-like landscape before her while she wrestled with her conflicting dilemma. Finding no answer in the gathering gloom, she turned her attention back to Crionna. "Please tell Granny that I am safe and sound and having a wonderful time in the fairy village. I will be home in a few days and can't wait to see her. I miss her terribly and send her all my love."

With this, Crionna bobbed her head and flew off into the night. Molly watched until she was out of sight, and then she went in to her own supper with Bumble and Clover.

Very early the next morning before the sun was up, Molly was still sound asleep in her bed when she was jolted wide awake by someone shaking her shoulders. "Bumble!...What's wrong?"

"Come on…roll out of bed, Sleepy Head. There's something ye have to see."

"Can it wait till daylight?" Molly groaned, turning over and attempting to pull the covers over her head.

"It will be too late. Ye have to come now."

"What is it?" Molly asked grouchily.

"It's a secret. Come on…I promise ye won't be sorry." Now Bumble was mercilessly tickling Molly's bare soles.

"All right!...I'm up. I'm up," Molly groused, throwing her pillow at Bumble.

The moment Molly stepped out onto the front deck, Bumble grabbed her around the waist and flew through the air, taking them past the edge of the village and a short ways into the forest. Molly was still wiping the sleep from her eyes when she felt the ground beneath her feet. "It's dark…I can't see anything," she said crossly.

"Sit ye down on the ground and just be patient," Bumble answered. Molly plopped ungracefully onto the ground…too late realizing that the ground was covered with dew. Her back end was now uncomfortably wet.

Within minutes, a small glow appeared on the horizon, and the sky began to slowly lighten. Molly could make out her surroundings enough to determine that they were sitting on the edge of a small meadow. "Bumble…what are we doing out here?" she whined leaning on her friend's shoulder and attempting to close her eyes.

Bumble pushed her upright. "Just one more minute…..There! Look at the meadow!"

As the morning mist dissipated and the sun rays struck the landscape, beautiful singing filled the air. It sounded as though a choir of angels was hosting a concert in the field. Bumble had Molly's attention now. She gazed about the meadow looking for the source of the heavenly music…and then she realized that the wild grasses that made up the meadow were covered with a million bright orange butterflies, gently flapping their wings. Her next realization startled her even more….it was these beautiful winged creatures that were doing the singing. With a surprised expression, she turned to Bumble who nodded to answer the unspoken question.

The girls sat without conversing for some time while the butterflies welcomed the morning's first light with their mystical song, and then as if they were responding to an unknown signal, they stopped singing and lifted into the air above the field. They swirled about like confetti being dropped from above and took flight, disappearing into the clear, blue sky.

Molly just continued to sit and stare at the sky in awe. "That was the most amazing thing ever! Does that happen every morning?"

"It only occurs once a year at the beginning of their migration. I happened upon it accidentally a long time ago, and I sneak off each year to see it. I think of it as my own personal secret, and I donna share it with many. I knew ye would think it grand as I do."

"I'm speechless….no matter how long I stay here, I don't think I will see all the wonderful pleasures your world has to offer. There is an unexpected surprise around every corner."

Bumble grinned in appreciation. "Come on, Molly May….my stomach is needing some of Clover's honey cakes for breakfast." With that, she snatched Molly up and flew back through the forest.

As they landed on the front deck of the house, they heard a shout from below. Peering over the railing, they caught a glimpse of four figures stepping into the village from the surrounding forest. Molly's heart leapt with joy when she recognized two of the figures. It was Elgin and Ronan waving in the distance. It had been several days since she had seen the guys, and she had been missing them terribly. Shouting back, Molly waved excitedly and headed for the stairs.

Chapter 25

Elgin closed the distance between them and grabbed Molly up, swinging her around in the air. When he set her back down on her feet, he did the same thing to Bumble. Ronan then picked up Molly and gave her a big bear hug. There were hugs and laughter all around between the four friends.

"Have ye two been fighting off all the handsome fairy gents the last few days?" Elgin asked with a cocky grin while casting a sideways glance at Ronan. It was apparent that the remark was intended to goad him, but Ronan's face betrayed nothing of his thoughts on the matter.

Bumble was quick to reply with her own jest. "Aye, our lips are sore from all the kisses we've had to hand out to keep the crowd of them happy."

At this, Ronan's face became a thundercloud, and Bumble punched him playfully in the arm. "Donna take on so, cousin. I've plenty of kisses left for ye." She puckered up comically and wrapped her arms around him while he leaned back with a grimace on his face, trying to avoid her lips.

Molly and Elgin roared with laughter at the two. "I donna think it's yer kisses he's a wanting," Elgin said.

"Aye, she kisses like a goat," replied Ronan.

"And how would ye be a knowing how a goat kisses, me dear cousin?"

Bumble's remark set the four friends to laughing once again, and Ronan threw up his hands in surrender. "Ye have bested me on that one. Please tell me that we are in time for the breakfast meal. We left early, and me stomach's gnawing me backbone."

"We were just hoping for breakfast ourselves, come on," Molly said, and they all headed to Clover's house.

A few minutes later, they were sitting down to a meal of blueberries and hot honey cakes fresh from the skillet. In between bites, the friends caught up on each other's activities for the last few days.

"We've come to take ye home to Hickory Hollow. There are four of us lads to escort ye through the forest. The other two are visiting their kin this morn. Granny says not to take any chances with the goblins still," said Ronan.

Bumble looked somewhat despondent at this news. "I was hoping ye would be staying longer, Molly."

"She can come back again, or ye can go stay with her and Granny in a week or two. There are always traders traveling through, and ye could join their group," Clover interjected into the conversation.

After breakfast was cleared away, Molly collected her things and strapped on her small backpack. She bid her hosts goodbye and thanked them for their hospitality. Bumble hugged her fiercely and whispered in her ear, "I'll come see ye and Granny in a few weeks and bring spider thread. Together we will weave it into the most beautiful cloth and have a seamstress make us some dresses that will make all the lads swoon…especially these two."

Molly, Ronan and Elgin met the other two young men in the center of the village and headed into the forest. At the edge of the town, Molly paused to turn and wave at Bumble and Clover who were standing on the front deck of the house perched in the tree. The sun had fully risen now, and shafts of morning light were beaming down through the openings in the overhead foliage. Bumble and her sister were lit as if by spotlight, and for the hundredth time, Molly wished for a camera so that she could capture such a visually exquisite moment. Instead, she memorized the scene and filed it away as she had many others, and then turned to join her fellow travelers.

Elgin took the lead on the path with Molly and Ronan walking side by side behind him. The other two young men bought up the rear. The men all carried bows on their shoulders and quivers full of arrows on their backs. Ronan explained that Granny had given them explicit instructions to be extra cautious. Ronan and Molly chatted as they moved through the forest for travel was easy on the well-worn footpath through the woods.

"I have truly missed ye, Molly May," Ronan said softly. "I hope ye will be staying home for a while now." With a captivating smile, he twirled the bracelet on her arm, pleased to see that she wore his gift.

"It was wonderful to visit the fairy village and get a chance to see how they live, but I am missing Hickory Hollow and all the villagers. I especially miss Granny. Has she been well these last few days?"

"Aye, she's as fit as a fiddle…but then she is Granny and has been the same all the many years I have known her."

Molly nodded, understanding what he meant. Granny was a fixture in the village. Everyone looked to her for advice and answers when problems arose. Molly supposed every village had old, wise folks that they looked to for leadership.

Ronan took her hand as they walked along and pointed out interesting foliage and flowers in the surrounding landscape. The flowers were bigger and taller here, since being so small changed one's perspective; therefore their scent was more powerful, also. It was a beautiful morning, and birds sang sweetly overhead. Molly thought she spotted Crionna sitting high up in a tree that they passed under.

A few hours into the journey, the travelers stopped for a break beside a stream. Molly took off her shoes and sat on the rocks with her feet in the water. One of their companions pulled out some roasted walnuts and shared his snack with all the others. Molly made a mental note to hand out the gifts for her friends that she had acquired at the Gathering. She would do that as soon as she reached the village.

After a short rest, the group was ready to travel further, and so they reclaimed their walking places and strolled on through the forest.

"Will it be much further, Ronan?" Molly asked.

"Tired already, Rua?"

"No…I just don't have any sense of how far apart the villages are in the forest."

Ronan glanced up at the sun and then at the shadows. "We should be there in time for the noonday meal."

Molly was beginning to get anxious to see the village she now thought of as home. She planned to visit Meadow and try her hand at spinning and weaving. She wanted to surprise Bumble when she came to visit, bringing spider thread. Molly was so deep in thought that she didn't realize that Elgin had come to a dead stop in front of her until she ran smack into his back.

"Hey....give a girl a warning...why don't you?" she protested.

The four men had quickly closed ranks around her forming a tight, protective circle. Their body language told her immediately that the relaxing morning had quickly taken a turn for the worse. Their backs were to her, and their bows were drawn. She peered under Ronan's outstretched arm, and what she saw caused her breath to catch and her heart to race.

Chapter 26

Molly and her companions were totally surrounded by goblins wielding wicked-looking clubs. The young men were facing 20 or more of the ugly creatures….not exactly good odds. Elgin thrust a large walking stick to Molly and said over his shoulder, "If they get past us, fight for all ye are worth, Molly Girl. Just like ye did before."

The words had barely left his mouth when the goblins sounded a battle cry and fell upon the elves. The young men fought valiantly. They shot arrows at the goblins in front and felled a few, but the fight became a hand-to-hand battle in a matter of minutes. Molly could see little at first with their tall backs blocking her view. An opening appeared when one of the men was overpowered by four goblins. Before the remaining three men closed the circle tighter around her, she glimpsed the young man throwing off one of the goblins and laying out another with a sound blow. It was apparent that all these men had been chosen to escort her home because of their brawn and expertise in combat.

Molly could see the skirmish clearly now as Elgin had been overpowered by several goblins and pulled away from the circle, but he was able to continue to throw punches very effectively. When Ronan was caught by a particularly nasty clout from a club and knocked to the ground, Molly saw red. With no thought other than saving her friends, she leapt into the fray of the battle and swung her stick with all her might. The goblin who had hit Ronan cried in pain as she connected soundly, and then she went after one of the brutes deviling Elgin. She hit him upside the head with such force from behind, that he never saw it coming and slumped to the ground, knocked out cold.

She saw that several goblins were lying about unconscious, and her four companions had regained their feet. Instinctively, all five fought their way into a position, once again, to protect each others' backs. It seemed the tide was turning in their favor, since many of the goblins had been disabled by the elves' fierce fighting. The goblins were mean and nasty, but they did not have the skill and strength of the elves. Molly's heart lifted as three more goblins fell by the wayside, but it quickly sank again when more goblins emerged from the forest and joined the battle.

Everything became a blur at that point. There was no way to defeat so many of them. Molly's fighting stick was wrenched from her hand, and she was grabbed by two of the goblins who dragged her kicking and screaming into the forest. When she managed to look back, her friends had disappeared under a pile of goblins, and she renewed her struggles with vigor. She bit, clawed, punched and kicked her captors until one goblin stepped up and blew a handful of powder into her face. As soon as she inhaled, she lost consciousness, and they let her slip to the ground.

"She had better awaken when we reach the cave, or Bruck will be in a foul mood," one of the goblins said in a growling, grunting voice.

The one who possessed the powder just shrugged indifferently.

"Since ye knocked her out, ye can carry her," said the other goblin, and they turned and headed through the woods.

The goblin left standing over Molly picked her up with a curse and slung her over his shoulder, striding off behind his cohorts.

The remaining goblins continued to fight long enough to give Molly's captors a head start, and then they began to fade away into the forest. The four young men lay on the ground semiconscious from the beating they had taken, and some time passed before help arrived.

Crionna had alerted Hickory Hollow to the goblin attack, and the elves had come running to render aid. They reached the fallen warriors after the fight and began to assess their wounds. One young man was hurt badly, and a stretcher was assembled to carry him back to the village. Elgin, Ronan and the remaining escort were badly bruised and had suffered cuts and scrapes.

"Help me find my bow and arrows," a stony-faced Ronan said to the crowd. "I'm going after them."

"Ye donna know where to look at the moment, and ye are in no shape to fight further. Ye body needs some mending," answered Bantry who had come with the villagers when the alarm had been sounded.

Ronan stood up abruptly as if to argue but then swayed on his feet in exhaustion. A tall elf shoved him back down onto the rock on which he had been sitting. "Ye won't make it far in yer condition. I understand how ye feel, but we'll get her back. We have to plan how to retaliate, and Crionna will know where they have taken her."

With this, the villagers gathered the wounded, young men and headed back the way they had come through the woods.

Later that evening, the entire village gathered in the center of town to discuss the situation. The first few minutes were spent letting the villagers express their outrage over the boldness of the goblins. The wise elders sat silent for a time, knowing that this venting of anger and fear was necessary.

Ronan sat white-faced....saying nothing but staring off into the forest. Finally, Elgin spoke up, "Why was Molly taken? She was carrying nothing of value that the goblins would want. They had planned this attack. This 'twasn't about stealing food as they have done in the past."

The crowd fell silent. Elgin had cut to the heart of the matter. When Granny spoke, she had everyone's attention. "Ever since we brought Molly here, the goblins have been unusually aggressive. There must be something they want from her. She is safe as long as they think she can give it to them. She is a smart girl and will buy herself time. Tonight we need to form a plan to rescue her. Crionna is tracking the goblins back to their nest and will be able to lead us there when the time is right."

Another villager spoke up, "Ye just tell us when and where, Granny. I have weapons aplenty to go around. That wee one that Molly rescued from the river at the Gathering could have easily been mine. I'll fight till I have none left in me to rescue that brave girl."

Cheers of agreement and support went up from everyone. Without knowing it, Molly had earned the love and respect of the entire village and had become one of them.

Elgin leaned toward the still, silent Ronan and gave his shoulder a firm squeeze. "We were outnumbered, Ronan, me friend. There was absolutely no way to stop them. We will get her back. Those nasty creatures donna stand a chance against our numbers. Take heart."

Ronan nodded wordlessly to indicate that he had heard his friend, but he did not respond and continued to stare into the dark forest as if he might catch a glimpse of her among the trees.

The town meeting went on late into the night, and it was well after midnight before anyone slept. In the hours before dawn, a large owl swooped through the village, perched on a windowsill and made soft hooting noises. In the dark cottage, Granny arose from the rocker where she had been sitting for most of the night and moved to the window. The two figures were mere shadows as they conversed quietly for a period of time, and then the owl took flight once more, disappearing into the forest. The old woman stood at the window and looked out into the deep woods long after she could no longer see Crionna.

Chapter 27

As Molly slowly regained consciousness, she realized two things right away. She was dreadfully cold, and she had a massive headache the size of all outdoors. She slowly sat up on the pile of straw on which she had been lying. It was covered by a moth-eaten wool blanket that smelled as though it had never been washed. As her eyes adjusted to the gloom, she took in her surroundings. She was in a cave that was dimly lit by small openings in the ceiling and torches several yards away attached to the walls. The chamber she occupied was a carved-out area off to the side of a larger room, and the entry way was blocked by thick vines that grew up from the floor to the ceiling and resembled the bars on a jail cell. Molly went over to the vines and tried to pull them apart, but it was useless. They were firmly in place. Next, she tried to squeeze through the space between them, but they grew too close together. Since escaping was not a possibility at the moment, she decided to get an idea of her surroundings.

She pressed her face between the vines and squinted in the faint light. The cave appeared to be a large, somewhat round room full of random items. There were tables set up in the middle to accommodate a large number of people with a few tables and chairs along the walls. Baskets, blankets, dishes and various items were scattered about on the floor with no thought to organization.

These goblins are a messy bunch. It looks as if they throw their pilfered goods about when they are done with them. She turned her head to see more of the room before her and winced in pain. Whatever they had used to knock her out had caused a wicked headache.

Her thoughts then turned to the young men who had been escorting her through the forest. Her last glimpse of them had been alarming as they had been desperately fighting but obviously losing. Maybe they had been taken, too, and were being held somewhere in the cave. Even though it hurt to do so, she yelled, "RONAN, ELGIN!....ARE YOU ALL RIGHT?"

She listened for several seconds, but all she heard was her own voice echoing back to her. She tried again many times and then surmised that they were not within the sound of her voice. She didn't know if that was good or bad news. If they were not captive also, then they would be coming after her….if they had survived the fight. That thought sent her into near panic.

She sat down on the pile of straw to think. She remembered how resilient the forest people were, how there had been no deaths that she had been aware of since her arrival and how they all lived far longer than the people from her world. She also remembered how quickly Ronan had mended from his arrow wound on the day she had first met him. These were encouraging details, and she planted the idea firmly in her mind that all four men were alive and being tended by Granny with her healing herbs and salves.

With her fears deliberately banished, she turned her thoughts to the puzzle of why the goblins had taken her captive. *Are they holding me for ransom? What do they want that they haven't already stolen in the past? The forest people don't use money.*

Perplexed, she continued to turn the questions over in her mind for several hours. She grew colder when the sunlight no longer came through the natural skylights in the ceiling, and only then did she realize that her dress was torn in several places. The neckline gaped from a long rent, and one sleeve was almost completely torn away, letting in the cold air. She wrapped herself in the thin blanket to ward off a chill and tried her best to ignore the smell.

Just then, she heard voices in the cave. The voices became louder, and she could see goblins entering into the large room. She sat very still, hoping not to draw attention to herself but to just observe and glean what information she could. They lit more torches, and Molly could see her surroundings much better. The motley crew seemed to be in high spirits and milled about for several minutes before settling around the tables to feast on baskets of food that were carried in by obvious lackys.

They were as hideous as Molly remembered, and their table manners were nonexistent. They dipped into the baskets with their ugly claws and fought over portions even though there seemed to be enough to go around. They smacked and chewed with their mouths open and belched loudly after they downed mugs of drink. They were especially proud of two barrels of stolen apple mead that had been carried in and tapped for the evening.

Listening intently, Molly could make out snatches of stories relating the details of the raid they had made on an unsuspecting village and the plunder they had taken. Tonight's feast was evidence of their thievery, and Molly's anger toward the goblins grew as their delight in taking advantage of the hard work of the forest people became more evident.

When most of the food had been consumed, the goblins filled their mugs once more and sat conversing, picking their teeth and laughing raucously. By this time, Molly had detected a pecking order within the clan of goblins. Their leader was called Bruck, and he stood a head or so taller than the others. He sat at the head of the table and was given first choice of the food in the baskets. The goblins sitting nearest him refilled his mug several times from the barrel and tended to his every need. Anyone becoming too loud or approaching too closely to the leader received a thump to the head or a well-placed kick that was brutally effective in keeping a semblance of order within the unruly mob.

Bruck spoke to the goblins nearest him, and two of them left the table, crossing over to where Molly was being held. As they peered at her through the vine bars, Bruck mumbled some words and waved his hand. The vines moved apart, creating an opening that the two goblins stepped through. They grabbed her roughly by the arms, pulling her up and through the opening. She was marched to the table where Bruck sat and was pushed down onto a chair to his right. Bruck motioned to one of the others, and a plate of food was slid in front of her. Molly had resolved to remain silent and uncooperative with her captors, so she just stared down at the plate and sat unmoving.

"Eat, girl, and then we will talk," Bruck growled at her.

Molly ignored his command and continued to stare down at the table. The goblins fell silent and watched in interest at her refusal to acknowledge their leader. With one swoop of his hand, he sent the plate of food flying and bouncing off the wall.

"I donna care if ye eat or not as long as ye give me what I want, Galeing....ye are the Galeing that we seek...are ye not?" With those remarks he grasped her chin and forced her to look at him face-to-face. Molly stared directly at his hideous face, determined not to show fear or distress. She let her anger crowd out any feelings of fright, and she glared boldly into his eyes. Her cold confrontation of their leader caused the other goblins to shift nervously in their seats. Bruck, on the other hand, seemed pleased with what he saw.

"Aye, ye are the one. Yer eyes have the mark of magic."

At this the goblins hissed, "The eyes...she has the eyes..."

Molly continued to stare unwavering...taking in his yellow teeth, long nose and overly large head. His lips pulled back into what Molly could only surmise was a smile.

He was used to others cowering in his presence, but the Galeing was not the least bit intimidated. He uttered a command that Molly did not understand, and all but two goblins left the room. His two minions took up positions behind Molly. The goblin leader leaned back in his chair, elbows on the arms and fingers intertwined. He cocked his head to one side, and his eyes gleamed as he spoke in a commanding voice, "Ye possess the magic of the crossing, and ye will give it to me."

Molly stared back down at the table in her previous uncooperative manner and remained silent. Bruck continued to speak in growling tones, "I know ye have the magic. Ye have been to our world several times in the past, and ye come through the doorway at will. Give it to me, Galeing, ...or ye and yer friends will suffer greatly."

With his last remark, Molly raised her head, looked directly into his face, and with a contemptuous look on her face, she slowly and deliberately shook her head. The ugly goblin leader roared in anger, and with one motion, shoved to his feet and backhanded Molly across the face. The force of the blow knocked Molly backwards out of the chair, cracking her head on the floor where she lay in a crumpled heap...unmoving. One of Bruck's flunkies leaned over her and then straightened up. With obvious nervousness, he spoke hesitantly, "I think the Galeing is dead."

Chapter 28

"If she is not dead, then she will soon wish she were," Bruck snarled. Just then Molly moaned and moved slightly. "Take her back to the holding chamber. I will give her time to regain her senses, and then I will get the magic one way or another."

One of the goblins picked her up and dumped her unceremoniously on the pile of straw in her cell once more. With a wave of Bruck's hand, the vines closed back into place. Molly lay very still, feigning unconsciousness so that she could eavesdrop and perhaps learn something of value. Her head hurt tremendously, since she really did hit it rather hard on the floor; she grit her teeth and fought back a wave of nausea.

Please don't let me have a concussion...or something worse.

The three goblins were arguing among themselves, and she strained to listen.

"Perhaps she donna have the magic, Bruck."

"It is her. I know it. Her eyes give her away. No other Galeings have been able to cross back and forth between the worlds. She has the power."

"What will we do if the elves come for her? They may want her back."

"What for?...Why should they care what happens to her? She is a Galeing and not of their kind....besides, once I have the magic, I will be the most powerful being in the forest. The village people will be helpless."

"Ye will become lord and master of the entire forest, Bruck," one of the goblins simpered.

Bootlicking toad...

Bruck roared with laughter at the flunky's last remark. "Lord and master of this world is just the beginning. With her magic added to mine, I can cross into the Galeing world. Just think of the riches we will find there."

Molly suppressed a shudder. The idea of the goblins in her world was unthinkable. So that big, ugly Bruck thought she had the ability to use magic…that was an interesting notion. Maybe she would be able to use that to buy some time for herself. Surely by now Granny and the others would know something had happened to the five travelers on their way home. They had been due in Hickory Hollow at noon, and it must be well past midnight. For the hundredth time that day, she prayed for the safety of her friends and escorts who had been attacked by the goblins. As she lay exhausted and shivering, she slipped into an uneasy slumber and did not awaken until the sun was high in the sky and the light was beaming once again through the skylights.

Her headache was somewhat better this morning, and since she had no dizziness or blurred vision, she assumed there was no major damage to her skull or brain. She got up slowly from the pile of straw and experimentally stretched her muscles. Everything seemed to be in working order despite her physical confrontations with those horrid creatures. She pressed her face in between the vines and looked about the large cave room. Snoring goblins lay haphazardly on the floor that was littered with overturned mugs and remnants of dinner. Molly hoped that they would sleep well into the day and leave her be. *Maybe they will all have nasty hangovers.*

She attempted to remember the words that Bruck had uttered when he had made the vines open. She tried several phrases and even imitated the manner in which he had waved his hand. Nothing worked. She paced about her small cell looking for something to use for a weapon, but other than the blanket, there were only small pebbles. She sighed heavily and sat back down on the pile of straw. She found a small, sharp rock and idly scratched on the rock floor to pass the time. A while later when that activity grew tiresome, she tossed the small rock through the vines at the nearest slumbering goblin. It bounced off of his large nose, and he grunted in his sleep, rolled over and resumed his clamorous snoring. Molly's tiny smile of satisfaction was short lived. Drawing her knees up to her chest, she dropped her head onto her crossed arms and settled down to wait for what would happen next.

Thoughts of her family rose up in her mind, and she wondered what they would be doing now. Had they finally stopped searching for her? Would her brothers all be off to college? Had they closed up the summer house and returned to the city? She knew her father would be missing her, but how would her mother feel?...Relief to finally have Molly's father all to herself since the house would be empty of children?

She then thought of Granny, Bumble, Thistle, Elgin and finally….Ronan. When his face came to her mind, she felt her wrist for the bracelet that he had given her…grateful that it was still there and had not been lost in the struggle. How badly had he been hurt in the fight? How long would it be before she saw him again? What type of magic did the goblins have, and could they use it to harm her friends when they came for her? Hours passed as these thoughts chased each other in her mind.

"Hooooooo…" The sound was soft and low, and Molly wasn't sure she had actually heard it. "Hoooooooooo..." There is was again. She lifted her head and looked about. She couldn't spot the source of the sound. Just then dried grass and dust sifted down through one of the skylights over her chamber. Molly looked up and saw Crionna's face peering back at her. Her heart soared with excitement, and it was all she could do to suppress a smile. Crionna's presence meant that her friends were not far behind, and she certainly didn't want to notify the goblins of that fact….better they were caught off guard. She nodded to her old comrade, and Crionna's head disappeared.

There was a racket in the cave, and Bruck and his flunkies came shambling into the large room. Any sleeping goblins deemed in their way were rudely awakened with kicks and scuffs. Bruck made his way to his chair and barked to one of his attendants, "Bring me the girl!"

Molly was once more escorted from her holding cell and brought to stand before the goblin leader. "This is ye last chance to give me the secrets of yer magic, Galeing, or I will take it by force."

"Maybe we can make a trade. I, at least, should get something out of this if I am going to hand over my secrets. It's only fair," Molly said attempting to put a sly look on her face.

Bruck leaned back in his chair and smirked. This was more like it. "What type of trade?"

"What of value do you have to offer? You already know what you want from me…make an offer, and we will negotiate."

"I can give ye Slade here," and so saying he thrust a particularly stupid-looking goblin in her direction and then roared with laughter at his own joke. The entire goblin pack hooted and cackled with glee…except Slade, of course, who ducked his head and slunk off to a corner. Molly almost felt sorry for the dull-eyed creature who was obviously the butt of many jokes.

When the noise died down, she gave their leader a look of disdain and said, "You don't have anything of real value, do you?"

Bruck narrowed his eyes and picked his teeth with a long curved fingernail. After several seconds he sneered, "What do ye know about goblins? Ye know nothing of our world."

"Well, I don't see anything in this trash heap of a dwelling that is of any use to me. So maybe you have some magic that might be worth trading for some of mine."

His big rubbery lips slowly stretched into a smile as if amused. "Why should I trade with ye….when in a few minutes ye will be telling me all I wish to know?" As he was uttering these words, he dipped his long fingernail into a small vial on the table and leaned forward without warning. His false smile had not prepared Molly for what came next, and she had no chance to recoil from his touch. His fingernail scratched a deep horizontal line along her exposed collar bone, and within seconds it felt as if her shoulder were on fire. It was all she could do to not cry out as the pain continued to intensify.

"Take her back to her chamber, and let me know when she is ready to talk. It won't be long….these Galeings are fragile things. She will be begging for me to take away the pain very soon."

Molly did not resist as she was hustled back to her chamber. She was in so much pain that she was only vaguely aware that Bruck had not closed the vines back into place. It didn't really matter. The pain was spreading from her shoulder and down her arm. It was all consuming, and she writhed on the pile of straw, hearing herself moan involuntarily. Mercifully, she blacked out from the agony and drifted in and out of consciousness, floating in a place where time did not exist and she could no longer hear her own sounds of whimpering. She also did not hear, when sometime later, the goblins sounded a cry of alarm and cries echoed throughout the cavern.

Chapter 29

Granny replaced the washcloth on Molly's forehead with a cool one. The young girl was bathed in sweat, and she moaned incoherently from time to time. Granny smoothed her hair back from her glistening face, murmuring soothing words as she did so. She looked at Ronan, noting his anxious expression and once again tried to ease his fears, "Go home and get some sleep…ye are worn out, and I'll not have two of ye needin' my attention at the same time. If there is any change, I'll send Crionna to peck at yer window."

"I'm not leaving her, Granny." And that was that. Ronan had had little to say since the villagers had returned with Molly. The attack on the goblins had been well planned and executed with the villagers outnumbering the goblins by far. Crionna had informed the inhabitants of Willow Grove Village of the impending battle, and the fairies took flight to join forces with the elves. The goblins never really had a chance. They had sorely underestimated the forest people's attachment to Molly and had failed to realize how tired the villagers were of their thievery and harassment of late. The goblins that had survived had been those that had scattered when the battle had first begun. The ones who had stood and fought had not been so lucky…some had been only injured…others fatally so.

Ronan and Elgin had been at the forefront of the attack and had fought brutally through the throng of goblins in the cave. When they had reached the chamber where Molly lay unconscious and had seen her physical condition, they had responded with a determined ferocity. Ronan had scooped her up and headed back through the cave. Elgin had cleared a path in the battle by swinging his fighting stick like a mushball bat, bashing the heads of hapless goblins that were unable to get out of the way. When the rest of the warriors had seen the limp and unconscious Molly being carried by their tall, white-faced friend, they were incensed and fought with renewed vigor until no goblins were left standing. Those who had attempted to escape into the forest, were chased by fairies who pelted them from the air with rocks from sling shots. Howls of pain could be heard all through the forest, and it was evident that the goblins would be hard-pressed to find a hiding place anytime soon. The contents of the cave had been set ablaze, discouraging any goblins from returning to take up residence. It would be a long time before the goblins would be a threat again.

While the warriors dealt with the goblins, Ronan, Molly and Elgin headed for Hickory Hollow escorted by three men who would serve as bodyguards, should they encounter any trouble along the way. Ronan carried Molly in his arms and refused Elgin's offer of help as they moved swiftly through the forest. Molly stirred once briefly. Her eyes opened slightly, and she looked up at Ronan. "I knew you would come for me," she whispered before closing her eyes and drifting back into unconsciousness.

The men reached the town in record time and were met by Granny and the women folk who had been waiting anxiously at the edge of the town, and keeping watch for their return. Granny's face had taken on a tight look when she saw Molly, and she wasted no time in having her taken to their cottage where she could examine her and apply healing herbs. She had shooed the men out and with Thistle's help, had cut away the tattered dress and had washed and tended Molly's cuts and bruises. The festering cut on Molly's collarbone worried her the most, and she used her most powerful salves to treat that area. Thistle helped Granny spoon liquid into Molly's mouth, and they managed to get an ample dose of the medicine down her. After dressing her in a clean gown and covering her with warm blanket, Ronan was allowed back in to sit by her bedside where he hovered now, silently gazing at her face.

Much of the town had taken up residence outside Granny's cottage and was awaiting news of the sick girl. When dusk settled upon the town, Granny stepped outside, gave a report of Molly's condition and sent the villagers home. The crowd that dispersed into the gathering gloom was especially subdued, for most had become quite attached to the young woman.

It was a long night in the old woman's cottage. Molly suffered through fever and chills…shivering with cold one minute and sweating profusely the next. Ronan and Granny took turns bathing her face with cool cloths and covering her with blankets when her teeth chattered. She awoke in the hours before dawn and clutched the old woman's hand. "It hurts, Granny!" she said, and tears slipped from the corners of her eyes onto her pillow as she writhed in pain. With Ronan's help, Granny succeeded in coaxing Molly into drinking a concoction that relieved her agony, and she finally slept peacefully for several hours.

"Those despicable goblins poisoned her with something vile, and her body's fighting to overcome it. If she were an elf, she would already be on the mend, but Galeings are much more delicate. I fear the situation is grim."

As Ronan added more wood to the fire on the hearth, he patted Granny's shoulder. "I know ye are doing all ye can, Granny. She seems to be resting for the moment. Lie down and get some rest, and I will keep watch."

Granny nodded wordlessly and stretched out on her bed in the corner of the room. Ronan took up his position by Molly's bedside once more and continued his vigil all through the night.

Dawn brought no improvement in Molly's condition, and by midmorning there were visitors in the village. Crionna had informed the other communities of Molly's illness, and Aiden, Clover and Bumble had come in a hurry along with several others from the fairy village. Ronan was shooed out once again so that Bumble and Clover could help Granny tend to Molly. Fresh salve was applied to her cuts and scrapes, and a poultice was used on the worst cut that was now displaying red streaks fanning out from her shoulder.

Molly drifted in and out…sometimes recognizing her friends and sometimes not…often calling them by other names. She talked incoherently and gazed about with bleary eyes, not recognizing her surroundings before once again lapsing into fitful sleep. It was evident to everyone, especially Ronan, that she was getting worse.

Granny and Aiden talked for hours…going over recipes for medicines and comparing notes on healing herbs. They tried several different poultices on the infected cut, but nothing seemed to override the effects of the goblin's poison. The wizened, old healer, Garth, from the gnome village arrived after the noon hour, and all three put their heads together and conversed in low tones for an interminable amount of time. That night, Ronan and Bumble took turns sitting by Molly's bedside with Elgin keeping his usual post outside by the door. When Molly became unusually fretful and restless in her sleep, Ronan stroked her hair and whispered, "I'm here, my `Alainn Rua. I will always be here. Ye are home now and safe with those who love ye."

Lying on a pallet in the dark corner of the room, Bumble could see his face and hear his tender words, and she quietly wept for her friend who had come into their lives quite by chance and had stolen her cousin's heart. It was a long time before she slept, and in the morning, Molly was alarmingly weaker than before with no hope for improvement.

The day dawned with gloomy, overcast skies that threatened rain and matched the mood of those assembled in Granny's cottage. Aiden, Garth and Granny had come to a consensus regarding Molly's situation, and they made the announcement to her friends. Granny's face showed exhaustion, but her voice was strong, "Molly will not last much longer, and we have done all we can. The infection that she is fighting has too strong a hold on her. The only way we can hope to save her….is to return her to her world. She told me often that her father was a great and learned healer. She is a Galeing, and she needs Galeing medicine. If she stays here, then she will surely die. By returning her, she has a chance to live."

"Is there no other way?" Bumble asked in an anguished voice.

"No…'tis her only hope," Aiden replied gently.

To Elgin, Granny said, "Take some men into the forest and retrieve Molly's clothes that she wore the day we found her. They are hidden in a hollow tree. Crionna will show ye where." Elgin nodded soberly without comment and did as he was directed.

As the others bustled around making preparations, Ronan knelt by Molly's bedside and took hold of her limp hand. With tears slipping down his face, he leaned forward and pressed his cheek to hers and whispered in her ear, "Return to me one day, my Rua." He then straightened and slipped unnoticed out the door and disappeared into the foggy drizzle.

Chapter 30

Molly sluggishly opened her eyes and stared dully at the white-tiled ceiling. Her parents' anxious faces came into view, hovering over her, and she blinked several times trying to bring them into focus.

Her father spoke gently and attempted to smile, "You're safe now, baby. You're in the hospital, and we're taking good care of you. Everything is going to be all right."

Before she could form an intelligent thought, she was asleep again, and it was another 24 hours before she opened her eyes once more. She slowly came awake to the sounds of mechanical clicking and beeping. She turned her head…amazed at how much effort that took, and looked around. An IV machine on a slender pole was the source of the annoying sounds. Beyond that, she could make out the slumped figure of her dad sitting upright but asleep, with his chin on his chest. "Dad…," she managed to croak.

His eyes flew open immediately, and he was at her side in an instant. He leaned over her and stroked her face. "What is it, baby?" He looked older than she remembered as if he had aged ten years since she had been gone. She searched his eyes for anger or irritation, but all she found there was concern.

"I missed you so much," she managed to whisper, and as she slipped back into the land of dreams, her father wiped his eyes and touched the auburn curls that fanned out on the pillow framing her deathly pale face.

It took several days for Molly to regain enough strength to talk…much less to raise her head off the pillow. Every time she opened her eyes, one family member or another was keeping vigil at her bedside. More often than not, it was her father. *He must be living here at the hospital, but that's not unusual. He's done that before with very serious cases.* Her brain was too muddled and confused to realize that this time she was the serious case. In these short waking moments, she said little but memorized her family's faces....afraid that she would awake the next time alone and in a strange place. She had lost all sense of time...sometimes when she opened her eyes it was light outside....and other times dark.

Finally, the day arrived when she was strong enough to sit up, and her mother adjusted the pillows so that she could sip juice from a straw. "Any chance of getting something to eat?" she asked her mother. Before her mom could answer, her dad came into the room, wearing his stethoscope around his neck, and it was obvious that he had been making rounds in the hospital. He stopped at the foot of Molly's bed, crossed his arms over his chest and cocked his head as he regarded her critically.

"Look who is sitting up and asking for something to eat," her mother said proudly.

A slow smile spread across her father's face. Without taking his eyes off Molly, he said to his wife, "Find a nurse and order a tray to be sent up right away."

After her mother left the room, her father became all business and gave her a thorough examination. He peered into her eyes and ears and listened to her breath with his stethoscope. He examined the cut on her collarbone and pronounced it healing adequately. He sat on her bed and held her hand as he spoke, "You had us all worried, honey. When we found you in the forest, you were running a high fever and suffering from a bad infection. It took the strongest antibiotics available to fight it, and even then, it was touch and go for a while. You are going to be weak for some time, and you'll have to stay in the hospital a few more days. When you do go home, it will be total bed rest so that you don't relapse....but you are out of the woods now, sweetheart."

With that last statement, it all came flooding back in an instant. Molly did not know whether to laugh or cry at the ridiculous accuracy of his last remark. Yes...she was back home in her world, but her memory of the village and its people were crystal clear in her mind. "I'm sorry for all I put you through, Dad. I didn't mean to be gone so long…I tried to get back, but I couldn't. I can't believe you were searching for me in the woods after so much time. How did you know I would still be there?"

Her dad looked confused for a split second, and then he said gently, "We found you on the fourth day. Half the town turned out to help us, and the local sheriff's office at Wells Point called in reinforcements from surrounding communities. We must have walked past that tree a hundred times during those four days, and then one day, there you were….unconscious and lying at the base of it. We think that you were constantly moving through the forest, and our paths did not cross until you collapsed and stayed put. You've been through quite an ordeal. It's not surprising that you are disoriented, and things will be confusing for a while. You probably won't remember much of what happened. The important thing is that you are safe now and on the mend."

A nurse entered at that moment bringing a lunch tray, and they had no chance to talk further. While Molly ate, she thought about what her dad had said. Four days…it didn't seem possible…but then again, she remembered what Granny had told her. Even though the two worlds existed side by side, time worked differently for each. She made it through half of her meal before exhaustion overtook her, and when her parents glanced over, they saw that she had fallen asleep holding her fork. Gazing at their youngest child, the husband and wife embraced each other, and Molly's relieved father said, "We have her back…our baby is home, and she is going to be okay." The wife said nothing, but her face was thoughtful. She had questions that no one else had thought to ask.

As Molly recuperated in the hospital, she turned many things over and over in her mind. She vaguely remembered being back in the cottage with Ronan, Bumble, Elgin and Granny being around her. She even remembered hearing Aiden's voice, and at one time it seemed Thistle and Clover had been there, too. Her thoughts were all jumbled, and she spent hours trying to sort them out. She had fuzzy memories of being carried in Ronan's strong arms while following Elgin's broad back in the midst of a battle that raged around them. Bruck's face came to her in her sleep, giving her nightmares, and she awoke at times with a start, her heart beating frantically. Her mother would appear at her bedside and talk in a low voice, reassuring her that she was safe until she fell asleep once more. Molly was withdrawn and reflective throughout much of her recovery, and her family worried about her mental state as her body continued to mend. She forced a smile when her brothers came to visit and tried to relieve everyone's anxiety. *Haven't I worried them enough?*

The day finally came when she was released from the hospital, and her excitement was dampened when she realized that they were going home to their city house and not the summer house which had been closed up for the season. Her mother pushed her wheelchair toward the elevators and pressed the down button. She then stepped back to the nurses' desk to speak to them one last time, leaving Molly momentarily.

"I think this belongs to you, miss. I found it on the floor of your room. It must have dropped out of your things as you packed." The young nurse assistant dropped something into Molly's hand and walked away.

Molly stared at the object for several seconds before recognition dawned on her. It was the metal bracelet that had been a gift from Ronan. Now, it was too small to be a bracelet but too big to be a ring for her finger. She closed her hand over it as her mother returned to her side. "What's the matter?" her mother asked in alarm when she saw the tears coursing down her face.

Molly shook her head…unable to speak for several minutes. "I guess I am just so glad to be going home," she lied, as the elevator doors slid opened and they entered for the short ride down.

Mark was waiting at the front door with the car, and he drove while her mother rode in the back seat with her. Molly was strangely quiet as she gazed out at the passing city. Everything looked so strange…bright and shiny….filled with the overwhelming sounds and the continuous movement of city life, impossibly tall buildings and crowds of people on the sidewalk…so different from the peaceful forest with its cool breezes, twittering birds and large interwoven branches overhead that formed a natural ceiling. Molly leaned her head back on the seat and closed her eyes to the scene that was rushing by outside the window. Her mother cast quizzical looks in her direction during the ride home, but for the most part let her ride in silence.

Chapter 31

Her father had not exaggerated when he had mentioned total bed rest. Her brothers saved her from mindless boredom by entertaining her with games and conversation every day. They even took turns eating lunch with her in her room as she was only allowed out of bed for visits to the bathroom. They were all so sweet and kind, and it was evident that they had lived through four days of hell while she was lost in the woods and had gone out of their minds imagining the worst. To have any time alone, she feigned sleep and allowed her mind to wander back to her friends in the village hidden deep in the woods. What would they be doing now? Surely they knew she was safe. Her rescue had to have been orchestrated by them. Hadn't Granny said that the magic would send her back when the time was right? Had anyone been hurt in the fight with the goblins? She prayed that no one had suffered serious injury on her behalf…that worry weighed heavily on her mind. She grew despondent with the idea that any of the forest people had died in battle trying to save her from the goblins.

When Molly's family saw her depressed state, they doubled their efforts to cheer her up with amusing activities and soon had her laughing in a lighthearted manner that was reminiscent of the old Molly they knew and loved. Her father took some time off from the hospital, and the family grew closer than ever in the following days. Coming so close to losing their youngest member had drawn everyone up short, and they clung to the remaining days of summer as if they would never come again….. for in reality, the family would not be together again for some time.

In a few short weeks, the boys would all leave home, and Molly would be left behind with her parents to complete her remaining years of high school. The time Molly's family spent together was bittersweet, and she knew they had all turned a corner in their lives. Her brothers were no longer children, and neither was she. They had all left their childhoods behind, and soon she would follow her brothers in leaving the nest.

All too quickly the day arrived when it was time for her brothers to depart, and they hugged her fiercely at the front door. Mark embraced her the longest and added these words of admonishment, "No wandering off, little sister. You are quite talented at getting lost, and they will kick me out of medical school if I have to come home and search for you in the middle of the year."

Molly promised him she would stick close to home, and she stood with her parents in the driveway and watched until their cars disappeared down the street. The house seemed strangely quiet, and she struggled to fill the silence with conversation that night at dinner with her parents around the table. Her father patted her on the back as she headed up to bed after dinner, "I am so happy to have my two best girls to keep me company around here. Don't fret, baby. Soon you will be back at school, and you will be so busy the days will fly by. Thanksgiving will be here before you know it, and the boys will be home for the holidays…you'll see."

Molly smiled at both her parents in what she hoped was a reassuring manner and headed upstairs to her bedroom. Tired and still slightly weak, she paused on the landing for a moment. She heard her parents' voices from below and listened to the exchange between them.

"Did you notice the dark shadows under her eyes? I don't think she should start school just yet. I'm going to call the school and let them know that she will start a week late." It was her father's voice, and Molly could detect a note of concern.

"Whatever you think, dear. You are the doctor after all."

"I'm going back to work tomorrow, but I want you to keep a close eye on her. She doesn't seem like our same, sweet Molly that went into the forest. I wonder what happened in those days when she was missing… I guess we will never know."

Molly could not hear her mother's reply, and she continued on to her bedroom where she wasted no time but promptly slipped into bed and fell into a deep slumber. Later that night, her mother softly opened her bedroom door and stood for several minutes, watching her sleep. As she turned to go, she heard Molly mumble something. It was obvious she was dreaming and talking in her sleep. At one point she clearly called out, "Ronan," and her mother stiffened with her hand on the doorknob. When Molly said nothing further, her mother left closing the door quietly.

In Molly's dreams she was dancing at the Gathering with a young man with dark, curly hair and laughing eyes who twirled her about until they both collapsed breathlessly on their backs in a sunny meadow of wildflowers and orange butterflies. When he pointed out a soaring bird high in the sky, she shaded her eyes and saw that it was the familiar shape of an owl. The owl glided closer on outstretched wings and came to rest on a branch of a nearby tree that was already occupied by a fairy with short, blonde, tousled hair, wearing a yellow dress and whose iridescent wings fluttered gracefully in the sweet-scented breeze. The dream quickly faded the moment she awoke in the morning.

With her father's return to work, the house did become unbearably quiet and lonesome. One rainy day while her mother was out running errands, Molly roamed the house….bored and at loose ends. She had watched enough television and had read enough books to drive a person mad, and she still wasn't allowed to leave the house yet. She climbed the stairs to the attic, thinking she would go through a box of old photos stored there. Her plan was to put together a scrapbook for her brothers that they could all enjoy when they returned home for Thanksgiving in November. While digging through cardboard boxes and trunks of old clothes, she happened upon a thin, cracked leather satchel. Curious as to what it might contain, she released the tarnished clasp and pulled out a sheaf of papers. She sat down on the dusty floor and sifted through the documents.

There was nothing much of interest until she came across a faded newspaper clipping from the *Wells Point Post*.

Mystery Baby Found in Forest

Two local residents of Wells Point, Tom Harris and Bob Johnson, discovered a small, female baby in the woods over the weekend while hunting. The baby was reported to have been lying in a woven basket under a tree and had attracted the men's attention with its laughter. The men immediately took the baby to the local community hospital, and the attending physician pronounced the child healthy and sound despite its apparent abandonment and exposure to the elements.

The sheriff's office is investigating this case and is perplexed regarding the infant's physical condition since evidence suggests that the baby had spent several days alone in the woods. There was nothing found on the scene to indicate the child's identity or the identity of the parents. Hospital authorities believe the baby to be about four months old and have reported the child to have a rare genetic condition that causes each eye to be of a different color. The baby girl also has auburn curls and a fair complexion with no notable birthmarks.

The sheriff's office has asked that anyone having information concerning this child to please contact the authorities. Meanwhile, Baby Jane Doe is being cared for at the community hospital, and the mystery of her identity continues to baffle everyone involved in the case. Equally puzzling is how the abandoned infant survived in the remote forest and was found in a healthy state with no signs of malnourishment. More details of this intriguing story will be reported as they become known.

Molly dropped the article in her lap and stared into space, trying to absorb it all. So many things now fell into place and made perfect sense. It was like the last piece of the puzzle of her life had been found and inserted to complete the picture. Of course she didn't look like the rest of the family…and her mother had always treated her differently from her brothers…now she knew why. Who were her biological parents, and why had they abandoned her? Molly supposed that she would never know the answer to that question. If they could not be found 16 years ago, then it would be impossible to find them now.

Her next realization opened more doors in her mind. The goblins had referred to her ability to cross back and forth between the two worlds and seemed to think she had done so more than a few times. To have survived as a baby in the woods, the forest people must have taken care of her until she could be found by other Galeings. Granny had said that the music had reached out and brought her back to them. At the time, Molly had thought that Granny was just referring to when, as a small child, she had followed the music into the woods and had briefly stumbled upon the elves celebrating with music and dance. Now she was filled anew with intense longing for the old woman who had unselfishly cared for her more than once and then each time had had to return her to the Galeing world. The irony of the situation was not lost on Molly. Her birth mother couldn't, or wouldn't, take care of her and had abandoned her. She was found by a mother who wanted her but who had to give her up twice to save her, and now she was stuck once again with a mother who had never shown any tender feelings toward her. If the whole sorry mess wasn't so painful, Molly would have laughed at the absurdity of it all. *Oh Granny, I do miss you so.*

There was no more time for reflection as Molly heard her mother's car in the driveway, so she hastily shoved the papers back into the satchel and returned it to its original place. She was downstairs in the kitchen when her mother came in the backdoor with sacks from the market. After helping her mother put away the groceries, she went back up to her room and spent the rest of the afternoon pondering what she had learned in the attic. That night she lay in bed, wide-awake, listening to the relaxing sound of rain on the roof, and she felt oddly calm and at peace for the first time since her return to the Galeing world.

Chapter 32

An hour before sunset the next day, the rain stopped, and the sun came out once more. Molly opened her bedroom window and pulled a chair close enough so that she could cross her arms on the window sill and rest her chin on her arms. She gazed out above the treetops, and in her mind's eye, could see Hickory Hollow and its inhabitants. She wondered if her friends had found their gifts that she had clearly marked with their names before she had left for the fairy village. She had packed them and sent them with Granny after the Gathering. She pictured Bumble wearing the green, soft leather slippers and Elgin in his beret with the bright red feather. *I bet he is strutting about thinking all the girls are ogling him.* That notion brought a smile to her face.

With the next thought, the smile faded as she pictured Ronan sitting alone on a boulder by a babbling brook and playing a sad, haunting melody on the flute that bore the carving of Misty Falls Village on the back. She closed her eyes and could almost hear the music drifting on the breeze that gently moved the curtains on each side of her. The words came back to her, and she hummed the last bit of a song she remembered....the song that was sung at the closing of the Gathering while candlelit lanterns twinkled overhead, and Ronan had put his arms around her as they swayed to the enchanting music.

"Should I reach deep woods again, I'll be forever there.
Aye, I shall be forever there."

Molly opened her eyes when she felt something lightly tickle her hand. A bright orange butterfly rested on her hand, and she smiled with joy at the sight of it. "Tell my friends in the forest that I am well once more and that I thank them for everything they did for me. Tell Granny that I remember everything she taught me. Take them my love and tell them that I will return one day if possible." A few seconds later, the butterfly took flight, and Molly lost sight of it in the sunset sky.

The next day, Molly heard her mother calling from downstairs. She leaned over the banister and looked down at her mother who was standing with her arms crossed, wearing a stern expression. "Come on down, Molly. It's time we talked."

Uh oh…this sounds serious. Wonder what I did this time?

When she reached the living room, her mother gestured to a chair. "Sit down. I want to know what happened in the forest while you were missing, and I want the truth."

Molly just gazed at her mother without comment. She had already decided that trying to tell anyone about the forest people would just land her in therapy…or worse…the loony bin, being forced to take high doses of anti-psychotic drugs to counteract her delusions. She would never tell a soul what had occurred.

"I want to know how your hair grew so much in the four days you were missing. Your father and brothers might not have noticed, but I certainly did…mainly since we had just gotten it cut," her mother probed.

When Molly maintained her silence and stared out the window, her mother's sharp voice continued. "Whatever possessed you to go wandering off into the woods like that? Since that time you got lost when you were three years old, we have warned you over and over. Was this a ploy to get attention? Your brothers explained that the camping trip was boys only."

But her mother was not done yet. "And who is Ronan?" At the sound of his name, Molly's head snapped up, and she realized her reaction had given her away.

"You talked in your sleep a great deal while in the hospital, Molly," her mother smirked. "Did you sneak off to meet some boy in the woods?"

Molly turned her face to stare out the window once more. There was really nothing she could say that would satisfy her mother.

In a voice rising with anger, her mother said, "You have a lot to answer for, and you will tell me what I want to know, young lady. There will be no secrets in this house!"

Molly slowly turned her head to regard her mother coolly. She could see that her mother was taken aback by her reaction…or lack of it.

In a very quiet, gentle voice Molly answered the woman that sat across from her, "Oh really? No secrets? Are you sure about that? Then tell me, Mother dearest…who are my biological parents, and when did you plan to tell me that I was adopted?"

You could have heard a pin drop…it was as if all the air had been sucked from the room. Her mother blanched, and her mouth moved wordlessly. Molly stared at the older woman unwaveringly…waiting for her answer. When her mother could finally speak, she sputtered, "How long have you known?"

"Does it matter?"

After a long moment, her mother sighed and answered in a tone of resentful resignation, "I suppose it doesn't. I wanted to tell you all along, Molly, but your father insisted that the truth be withheld from you. He was afraid that you would feel as though you didn't belong. He wanted you from the first moment he laid eyes on you, and when you were released from the hospital, he brought you home to the summer house at Wells Point."

When Molly spoke again, her voice was as quiet and gentle as before…and also a little sad, "Dad loves me, and I am his daughter despite who created me. The only one who has ever made me feel as though I didn't belong…was you, Mother. For a long time, I thought there was something wrong with me, but it wasn't me…was it? You could never love and accept a child that was not your own….much less one that had been abandoned in the woods, and Dad hasn't a clue. Don't worry. I love Dad too much to tell him. He doesn't have to know. It will be our little secret."

With that statement, Molly got up and walked out of the room. When she paused and looked back, her mother was sitting hunched over with her face in her hands.

From that day forward, an unspoken truce existed between the two. While her mother never became overly affectionate toward

Molly, she no longer criticized her at every turn, and their relationship was more amicable. True to her word, Molly never let her father know that she was aware of the details concerning her birth, and her mother never again questioned her about what had occurred in the forest.

Chapter 33

62 years later

Molly sat rocking on the porch of the summer house and gazed across the yard. It was rather lonesome without the kids and grandkids visiting. They had promised that they would try to come later in the summer before school started, but something told her that would not happen. They tended to come less and less these days, and she was starting to get too old to come up by herself and open up the house. Besides, the house was getting rather rundown and decrepit….kind of like Molly herself. Her once auburn hair was now faded to gray, and her face was lined with deep wrinkles and contained only hints of the girl she used to be. As she rocked, she thought back over her life and how it had turned out.

Following her brothers off to college as planned, she had earned a degree in business and then set out to do much more. She opened her own store, selling organic food, herbs and various homemade items such as reed baskets and hand-woven garments and had developed her own line of healing salves and poultices which had done quite well…well enough that she now owned 15 stores nationwide. Well…she owned them in name only, since she had turned over the running of the business to her children years ago.

Her children…they had made her proud. She had met her husband after college, and together they took a leap of faith and had invested everything into the first store…..an investment that had paid off. Her dear, sweet Mitchell had always believed in her and had always allowed her to dream big. He had never questioned her business decisions and had let her take the lead in running the store.

They were distressed when their attempts at having children failed, but Mitchell had agreed when she suggested adoption. They had adopted a girl and had named her Faith. It was only fitting…really. To their surprise, Molly became pregnant a year later and gave birth to a baby boy whom they named Ronan. A heart attack had taken Mitchell when he was only 45, leaving Molly to raise the children and continue running the company alone.

She never forgot the time she had spent in the woods with the forest people so many years ago. The memory was still strong and vibrant and fixed in her mind, but there had been no chance to return to that world again. Her brothers saw to that. They tackled her whenever she even looked in the direction of the forest that ringed the edge of the yard of the summer house. Once or twice she thought she spotted an owl sitting on a branch in the deep shade of a tall tree in the yard, but when she blinked, the branch was empty, and she couldn't be sure of what she had seen. Life took over after that, and in the following years, she was much too busy with her work and children to go wandering into the woods.

She and her brothers brought their own children to the summer house to spend time with their grandparents. Each summer, the house had overflowed with people and laughter. The children swam in the lake and biked into town just as she and her brothers had, and when dusk fell, they bunked on the screened sleeping porch, listening to the crickets sing in the dark.

Her parents and brothers were gone now, and her children and grandchildren were the only ones who came to the summer house anymore. She supposed that this would be the last summer…if anyone, besides herself, came at all this year.

In her mind, she could hear the sounds of long ago voices echoing in the empty rooms of the house behind her, and she could imagine her brothers playing ball in the yard once more and shouting to each other as they had done in those carefree days. A wave of nostalgia swept over her and left a feeling of sadness in its wake. She pulled a handkerchief out of her dress pocket and wiped a tear that had tracked down her face, following one of the many lines she now wore that was a sign of her age. *I'm an old fool…missing what was and what can never be again.*

She sighed and got up to go into the house to make a pitcher of iced tea. *What was that sound?* She leaned on her cane and stood very still, straining to hear it again. *Was that…it couldn't be…but it is.* Music was floating across the yard, and she walked slowly to the edge of the porch…and then she stepped onto the grass. A song was being played on a wooden flute, and the melody was hauntingly familiar. As she continued across the yard, a feeling of joy and excitement filled her soul, and she instinctively reached up and clasped the pendant that she always wore on a chain about her neck….a small, metal circle of intertwined vines that had been a bracelet so long ago.

The music grew louder, compelling her to step from the yard into the forest…and so she did. The shade under the trees was as cool as she remembered, and her pace quickened despite her need for the cane. Molly never looked back as the music wove its spell around her, and she placed one foot in front of the other, moving without hesitation, further…into the deep woods.

Epilogue

And just what did happen to Molly when she returned to the forest?

Perhaps, that is another story for another time and another place.

Made in the USA
Las Vegas, NV
06 September 2023